The Lesser Evil

A powerful novel set in the late Sixties

By

Victor John Tarry

Evil serves it's own purpose
Whilst it Succeeds it Carries A
Seed of Its Own Destruction

Second Edition 2012

Order this book online at www.trafford.com
or email orders@trafford.com

Most Trafford titles are also available at major online book retailers.

Printed in the United States of America.

ISBN: 978-1-4251-9111-5 (sc)
ISBN: 978-1-4251-9112-2 (e)

Trafford rev. 11/17/2012

www.trafford.com

North America & international
toll-free: 1 888 232 4444 (USA & Canada)
phone: 250 383 6864 ♦ fax: 812 355 4082

The Lesser Evil

This story is dedicated to my dear wife: Dawn, who inspired, encouraged and worked with me throughout the writing of this story.

I must also congratulate my daughter-in-law Georgina for correcting my errors and editing my work.

Thanks to Ann and Gary O'Connor for advice and Computer Graphic Artwork

And Samantha for her word processing skills.

The Lesser Evil

Contents Page

The police found Veracity Farm to be a hot bed of internationally organized crime with treachery and murder on the menu.

Once their thoughts did both ebb and flow,

As passion did them move.

Once did they breathe a lover's kiss

And then they were in love.

Then did they the flesh explore

And all the pleasures prove.

Then enlightened they swore,

To live together for evermore.

Introducing: Vic Brandon
Hero extraordinaire

The Lesser Evil

NEW IDENTITY

Victor Brandon was getting bored, that's not like him. His radio played but he hadn't the patience to listen to it. He thought to open a bottle of beer, also intending to make a sandwich then changed his mind. He looked at his watch, it was time for the local pub to open he mused and made himself ready to leave the soulless one bedroom flat in which he'd lived for many weeks, since he'd been discharged from the army. He was not used to civilian life yet, although he was endeavouring to understand it and fit in somewhere. He'd have enough money to buy food and drink, for not more than a few weeks. If he hadn't found gainful employment soon life could be bleak. He'd applied for many jobs, was optimistic, written many letters but industry was not interested in a long term serving spent soldier. Although he'd have worldly experience serving abroad in the various out-posts of the Bristish empire in the rank of sergeant, no place could be found for his disciplined natural ability to deal with men, rank and file. There were agencies to help ex-servicemen, not for him, no humiliating hand-outs. It had seemed exciting being part of a united nation's armed forces. At least the world was going in the right direction and he'd done something to help. He remembered as a boy hearing about the League of Nations, the British Empire being the greatest organisation in the world. There'd be no more war, they said but there was. Tragically there was!

The Lesser Evil

The United Nations was different. No nation could challenge such a great power. He was proud to be part of it. Nations bonding together in common cause, until it was realised not all nations bonded in unity and cause. Otherwise who were the gunmen infantry shooting at him? Who set the mines in the road along which he drove the army trucks just as it triggered a roadside mine exploding and propelling the wrecked truck and it's driver himself yards into an adjacent field? Although he was seriously hurt and retained in a field general hospital for many weeks, when finally discharged he was happy to learn that he was not permanently damaged. The war needed every able-bodied man and he was just another patched up casualty returning to duty. He'd missed some of the war though, whilst his comrades courageously and gallantly fought in depleting numbers. After four days of continuous fighting, what was left of their company had been demoralised, hospitalised or captured. There were reports that many died.

Vic had signed on to be a regular infantry man. He was a good soldier, full of the right spirit and enthusiasm, trained in the art of modern warfare. He'd believed in himself and the outcome of the war they'd be bound to win. They had the support of the empire with them. When it was all over he was an empty shell. He wondered just how much they and he had won. They'd taken his youth and squandered it on the battle fields. They gave him medals, said he was a hero and discharged him with an exemplary conduct, meagre pension and little money. These things counted for nothing in a country struggling to recover from ravages of war. He had to recognise that nobody wanted a spent soldier. Not now anyway. He was a civilian; he'd saluted for the last bloody time. He was alone and free, that was his only asset. All his thinking had been done for him, now he will have to learn to think for himself, for his future. He desperately needs to create a new civilian identity.

He glanced at his own reflection in a shop window as he walked to the pub, who would have taken him for a squaddie anyway? He was upright, well groomed and smart in appearance. He saw that as he walked to enter the 'Black Bull', a popular pub. He'd frequented many times before, just wasted his time and money on booze. The pub was already crowded, he stood back waiting, he wasn't in a hurry. Everybody seemed eager for drinks, pushing and nudging to be served first, he just stood aside looking. It's a rat race they'd brought to the boozer where they were supposed to relax. They were a people apart to him. He moved to give his order and a loud mouth called over his shoulder. "Two pints of best bitter, you don't mind old boy", the voice droned behind him. "We're in a hurry … there's a good man". He did mind but said nothing just looked at the person in contempt. Normally he would have told the rude bastard about his ancestry, thinking how ill-mannered, undisciplined and vulgar many people appear in the pub and in other walks of civil life he'd encountered.

He moved to a small bar and drank well alone and quietly relaxed. He could hear music in the other bar, loud mechanical jukebox music blues aroused him. The tempo like military music engulfed him. He remembered as a boy he'd followed the band, fell in, marched behind, he felt full of pride. He shuddered at the thought that grown men still hankered to follow the band to war. It was like some evil drug with a high death rate, yet that's what he did … He thought of times he'd just sat alone and drank, wondering, he felt something was missing in him, he was lost. Everything had changed and he hadn't changed with it. His soul seemed empty and yet he felt angry, mentally disturbed, not belonging anymore, like being in a void.

He walked out of the pub and into another and another. He was still walking after midnight. He felt tired and empty, empty. He cherished the night air that cleared his head, he thought about his future, something he had not done much about before. He was fit, alert, smart and healthy, there must be a place for him somewhere. The moon coming from behind a cloud effected and enlightened his mind, in an inspiration he believed that advertising in the local press will bring him future employment, he has much to offer. The following days he eagerly skims through the news sheets to read for himself the information he presented. He is self-disciplined, reliable, of good character. Seeks gainful employment in commerce or industry. Single male, 36, willing to travel, clean driving licence, and all offers taken seriously. It goes on to give his address and telephone number. He read the advertisement in the newspaper again, there seems to be nothing wrong with it but it's past midday of the second publication and nobody has phoned, neither had anybody called at the door, perhaps the following morning post will bring offers. He looked again there were many seeking employment, offering skills and qualifications. His heart sank, what hope would there be for him. He'd neither skill, trade or civil qualification, only basic general education, and Army education, Jujitsu.

He'd found human relationships difficult, all his life he'd been on the move, seen so many friends posted away, killed or injured and he'd learnt not to get too involved. Then after a time he'd got out of the habit of making friends. People thought him distant, unemotional, an uninteresting person. How could they know? Why should they care? Often he felt the need to develop a relationship with a woman. He'd seen himself in emotional, passionate affairs that raised his hopes and expectations. The army life was no place for a woman to bring up children therefore he'd promised himself not to get too involved, always kept his distance, no commitments, no propositions, no responsibilities.

He's desperately endeavouring to rid himself of his past military attitude and image. He sees new horizons appear, new dawns awaken, if only someone would respond to his plea for employment to give him a chance to put his feet on the first step to a creative civilian life. Anxiety builds within him anticipating a call, a knock on the door … anything, waiting is tedious, he knows he's waited many times; 'he also serves who stands and waits', he'd heard that said many times, typical army jargon.

The war was over. Hostilities ceased more than a year ago. Being an occupation army in Germany was often day after day monotonous, just waiting for something to happen. Regimental duties continued regardless. Sergeant Brandon was on duty responsible for security that day.

He was waiting when Judith arrived on the early morning shift, she was employed as an officers mess cleaner in the Army barracks in Hanover. She'd been cleared by a Denazification Tribunal. German civilian employed persons had to be booked in and out, that's how he'd met Judith. He'd watch her legs stride into the barrack guard room to record her arrival. She was a good looker, he followed her to the officers mess kitchen where she immediately made morning coffee for the officers and returned to offer some coffee to her admirer. He sat, offered her a cigarette, he lit it for her. "You're German aren't you?" he asked, obvious question, he might have been wrong.

"Half German, my father was a Polish Jew, I'm sorry", she said.

"What for, forget it, German, Polish, Jewish, it's all the same to me, for being a woman you need not apologise".

"Thank you", she laughed a little. "I'm not used to receiving compliments. I'm a working woman, I need the money to keep my self-esteem. I share a room with a friend" she said. "I wouldn't have it any other way, life for us is difficult now".

"I know ... but I want to know why ... do you have an inferiority complex?" She didn't answer.

She spoke perfect English with only a trace of an accent. He took more notice of her, she wore her dark hair short, like most women and her hazel eyes sat wide against her high cheek bones. She seemed to possess a certain vitality that made her attractive, yet she was neither beautiful nor pretty, perhaps more handsome of figure than face.

"How long have you been working here?" he asked.

"Four weeks".

"I've never noticed you before".

"I was frightened when I first came so I tried to be; how do you say, inconspicuous because I remember the Nazis, but here I find you're different, no persecution, no orders, no curfews".

"Were you afraid of the Nazis?"

"Yes they were horrible", she stopped, "I can't talk about that now I have work to do". She moved away.

"Tell me later I want to know".

"OK later", she said and took her things to leave.

"Where, later where shall I see you?"

"The Riverside Park by the barge quay at 3 p.m.". With those words she went about her work, she had a mature look as if she had seen a lot of life. There was a haunted depth in her, yet he supposed she would be no older than 23.

The Lesser Evil

TRYST

Sergeant Vic Brandon lay basking quietly in the hot afternoon sun upon the grassy gently sloping riverbank. The place was almost deserted and then she came as if from nowhere and knelt down beside him. He didn't move, he watched her shield her eyes from the sun. She heaved a breath of fresh air and felt free. "I've come here often, it's so peaceful here", she said after a pause. "I'm free, no fences".

"Stay then, I don't need to return to barracks until 6 p.m."

"It gives me … a sense of freedom". She sounded happy with those words; she had been behind barbed wire, but now she was on the outside of a double fence of barbed wire, she was experiencing a sense of liberation, no guards with guns watching everyone.

"You were going to tell me about the Nazis, you said they were horrible to you?"

"No, not now, it's too nice now, I don't want to spoil it. I'll tell you some time but just now I'm pleased to forget it".

Vic had often read and heard about the cruel way Nazis treated Jews and he understood she was still anxious and frightened, he wanted to take her away from the squalor and oppression she had known. Why should he care, but he did; he'd seen so much of it during the war, he was trying to understand her anguish. He stood up and helped her to her feet. They walked hand-in-hand as he lead her away around a bend in the river bank to a secluded place; he didn't look at her but he felt her hand gripping his tightly, meaningfully.

The river flowed quietly and the area was deserted, people rarely used it. They sat where the bank was shallow, gazing out across the expanse of water. All was silent, neither spoke. It was clean, fresh and pure, unbelievably different from the war torn atmosphere of the town, it allowed them to breathe. He looked at her, she was staring at the river flowing. "Thank you" she whispered.

"For what?"

"For bringing me here"

"It's as much for me".

"Is it?"

Suddenly she stood up, shed all her clothes and leaped into the water and he followed. They swam together in the warm water, lazily and silently they swam side-by-side, slow easy strokes. Then they lay on the grass with their bodies touching, the sun tanning their skin. It seemed to eat into their souls. It relaxed them and gave a sense of peace that neither had really known.

Other afternoons followed, each time they went to the same place each occasion he gave her a bar of chocolate.

"You're a chocolate soldier" she said with endearing eyes, "I love chocolate never had much in my life, thank you".

There were hours of simple intimacy, which developed a bond, between them and yet they had never kissed or embraced. They both knew it could not last. The fifth day together, that afternoon, the atmosphere was different between them. They knew it was the last time. They knew it had to come. They were both resigned to it.

He stood in the water waiting for her, he held her naked waist as she slipped in beside him. Suddenly time mattered. There was so little left. He wanted her physically, wanted her desperately. His arms tightened around her exciting body, she responded to him, gripping his shoulders as their bodies pressed together. They kissed, it was the spark to kindle their passion within them it was a desperately hungry kiss. A kiss of physical lust. A kiss that went through them urgently reaching to the depth of them. They were unconscious of everything except each other.

She wrapped her legs around his and they fell together, partly supported by the water, she moved her thighs against him probing, searching for his awakened sex. She leaned backward thrusting forward. He gasped when he felt himself tremble wildly. He kissed her savagely. She held him tightly and they stayed locked together. The water around them rippled and waves went out, out, out ...

They came from the water and lay gazing up at the clear blue sky. It was as if they were in a different world. Free of care or worry. He cupped and fondled her breast as she lay back with her head on his chest. It was easy for him to roll over to her. Their bodies blending perfectly as if they had been lovers for years and upon the grass bank they made love again. She was by far the best lover he'd ever had.

Their thoughts of their future gradually seeping back. The warm sun must have lulled him to sleep, suddenly he woke and she was looking down at him. Her eyes glistened.

"You look sad, have you been crying?", she stopped for a moment.

"I want to talk to you ..."

"Go on then",

"You know nothing about me"

"I don't need to ... this is only here and now you understand?"

"But I must tell you".

He stroked her black hair, she wanted to talk, he must let her, and he knew it was something in her that must come out, it'll ease her conscience.

"Will you listen ... try to understand?"

"I'll try, of course I'll try".

She heaved a deep breath, the emotion was gone, and she sadly told of her past as if it were a life's history.

She was born in Stuttgart Bavaria, her father had a small business, they were comfortable until Hitler came into power, and then feelings rose against them. Their ways were different, their religion was different, and people were afraid, suspicious or intolerant. The Nazis spread hate and bitterness, sanity was overcome, and bloodshed came in. The ordinary people looked on, and in doing so condoned it, or closed their eyes to it. When Hitler's armies took over everything, she was only twelve,

8

and her sister sixteen. A year later her sister was raped. Her father complained to the police. Next day sadistic Nazi savages came and smashed up the shop, and beat her father near to death without mercy. They would find pleasure in seeing Jewish people suffering; they were the superior race, sadistic monsters.

She was sent to live with an aunt, and never saw her parents or sister again. About a year later, her aunt was denounced and both were taken to a concentration camp. The camp commander took a fancy to her; she resisted and was ready to die. Her aunt persuaded her to yield and she become his mistress and for two years she lived with him until he was sent away. By then she was only known as a whore and sent to a soldier's brothel where troops queued to use her. She felt that she would never be clean again but was able to shut her eyes and her mind away from the degradation her body suffered. The swine gave her a venereal disease and she was sent to a special camp where doctors used her to experiment with various drugs. Time there stood still, it could have been three months or three years of sheer hell; she was numbed most of the time.

The Yanks came and released the prisoners and she got instant medical care and attention. The war was over, but life wasn't easy and food was scarce. The Yanks gave her food but she had to find her own shelter, often she slept nights under a railway arch. She made inquiries about her parents but got no results, she contacted a Jewish organisation helping to create the state of Israel in Palestine. It was like a dream, a new lifestyle, a country of her own. Nearly two years later her new life awaited her, many were as eager as she. She was still young and healthy if only the memory of those past years hadn't scared her forever; she heard that the waiting may soon end and that she might be going.

He was dumbfounded and humbled. He realised that she had poured out her whole story for the first time. It had all been contained inside her. The horror, degradation and inhumanity, she couldn't tell her own people, for they too had memories. They had also suffered. He didn't know what to say but felt very sad and lost for words; he just hugged her close with an ache in his heart.

"Sorry" she whispered, "for making you listen"

"You have nothing to be sorry about"

"You mean it"

"You had to tell someone and I was willing to listen"

"Yes you asked me to tell you"

She buried her face into his chest and kissed him. He didn't want to make a wrong move or hurt her, although he felt for her.

"Does it make any difference?" she asked.

"What?"

"That I was driven into" … she hesitates … "Being a whore?"

"Christ no …"

"It will to many people"

"Is that what you are afraid of?"

She didn't answer, but they talked until dusk, they spoke of their anxieties and their fears, they didn't really understand but they felt a mutual sympathy. They saw no future together. They had shared a love affair but neither mentioned the word love, yet, they'd enjoyed a fulfilment beyond most. He wondered if there was perhaps a military equivalent for love, and he'd found it? The days together, more like a brief honeymoon, had to end. Suddenly it was all over. There was no escape, no solution; they had to go their different ways, she to Israel in Palestine, he to the barracks … they had to go forward without each other …

The Lesser Evil

THE COMMISSION

Vic Brandon suddenly looked at his watch, 1530 hours. The newspapers had been on the streets since daybreak and nobody responded to his advertisement. He'd been let down; disappointed before, this was nothing new, only another situation to face up to. He lifted the newspaper from the floor and sat to read again. He's ready to give up. The telephone rings. It gives him a start; he was resigned to hearing nothing further that day. He thought perhaps this is it, an offer of a job.

"Mr Bwandon," said a man with a voice impediment I am reading your advertisement:- ex army, disciplined, reliable and willing to travel etc. is that you?" the male voice demanded to know, and spoke as if he'd been used to giving orders to subordinates.

"Yes that's right, that's me." He said in a confident, positive manner.

"Well now I've got a job for you, more in the way of a commission:- I'll explain:- My son had an accident whilst driving in Dusseldorf, Germany about two months ago. He left the scene, and his car was taken to a compound by the police. He is summoned to attend court, to answer charges; to pay the fine and recover his car, but he can't do any of these things. He is in an American university, and obviously cannot attend, and neither can I, since I am tied up in business here in Bournemouth. The job simply is this:- You go to Dusseldorf court tomorrow and deal with matters. I'll get all the documents to you soon. Get a release order

11

from the court, and drive the car back. I'll pay all costs and your fee in advance. Did you get all that?"

"Yeah I got it, but I don't understand it. Tomorrow you expect me to be in Germany to attend a court" before he could finish, the man interrupted.

"At 1130 German time, I'll make all necessary arrangements and get everything to you in about an hours time, by special dispatch, including your fee. How much?" he demanded.

"I'll want more details before taking a job on like this, at such short notice!" he was stopped again.

"Right, I'll spell it out to you. I'll arrange for you to be on a flight leaving Southampton airport, departure time 0730 tomorrow. You should be clear of Dusseldorf airport by no later than 10.00 hours, you will get a taxi to the county court, the taxi driver will know where that is, about a 30 minutes. Leave your car at Southampton airport car park on a 24-hour ticket; tell the car park attendant that you will be back very late the same day to get your car. The car you bring back to England you will leave in the place where your own car is parked. You will have a ticket for your flight; money for a taxi and other expenses in Deutch Marks, 2000DM; courts summons notice; and all relevant documents, including a letter authorising you to act on behalf of the accused, Thomas James Baker. The fine might be with a release order about 1000DM. Now about you're costs and fee?" He demanded. He spoke like some very efficient officer giving orders to troops.

"Mr Baker, what was your son doing in Dusseldorf anyway?" he enquired.

"He had intended to travel up with Southampton supporters club in their coach, to attend a match, Dusseldorf V Southampton. He got delayed, trouble with his girlfriend and arrangements to go to America. So he travelled later in his car to Ostend by ferry, and attending the match the next day. In the evening, while driving around the town, his car came into collision with another car, with four rowdy German football fans, each accusing him of causing the accident, and starting to push him about and insisting he had been drinking. He was unable to speak the language or defend himself. Upon seeing the police arrive he managed to get away.

12

He walked back to his hotel, suffering nothing more than shock. All the papers will be with you soon".

"Do you understand the situation better? Now your fee, how much?"

"Effectively I have started work on this job, and will want £200 per day, if I'm back tomorrow evening". He was stopped again.

"O.K. I see its £400 you want, you'll get it in hand soon. Time is of the essence. If you read all the information and need to ask questions, I'll phone you again about 7.30". The line went dead.

Vic wondered about this man, he seems to have a flair for organisation, with a commanding attitude. He is to expect a person to appear at his front door with documents to study; flight tickets; ferry-boat crossing reservation; itinerary and cash, Sterling and Deutch Marks, and no question of references. He's not worried about cash in hand, so can't lose out, but he can't help thinking about this caper. Why was it left to the last minute before contacting someone? He must have spoken to the court about it because the procedure was explained. He shrugged his shoulders.

He'd have to fulfil this task with all due diligence, it could be the making of a career, a starting point for future reference he thought, whilst packing a weekend bag with a few things; ready to leave in the morning. It would be a pleasure to see Dusseldorf again.

Suddenly there's a loud knocking upon the door. Vic hurries to open it.

"I'm sorry mate, the bell doesn't work, and I have an urgent package to deliver", he thrusts it forward. "If that's you, will you sign here receiving it?"

He signed accordingly, and took the package of documents inside to examine them. He found everything as promised, and correct; he counts out the bank notes in denomination and currency; the total added up. He studies the itinerary: - park your car in airport car park well in time to clear airport formalities to board the flight for Dusseldorf; it continues to give step by step details of every expected event; including the ferry-boat boarding time, and all necessary documents. Examining the documents he notices that they are all officially stamped 'Sunrise Travel Agents', he understands why everything was laid out so carefully now, but cannot help wondering why another agency in Germany was not asked to attend to the business? He dismissed the thought, it would work out much the same whichever way it was done. He'd always acted upon instructions and with military precision, he planned to leave his flat at 0500 hours the next morning, giving himself little time to pack the necessary apparel before departure.

It's a beautiful morning as he drives into the airport car park and is directed by the attendant to park his car in the corner earmarked for long stay parking and he is given a 24-hour ticket. After completing all documentation, clearing customs, and grabbing a coffee, he is seated in the aircraft bound for Dusseldorf. He began to feel more like a civilian for the first time since he left the army. He loved the attention the air stewardesses were giving him, and that he was treated with courtesy and respect; no longer a squaddie. His ego rose a little; he's now an important man on a special assignment. He smiles to himself and nods to the briefcase upon his lap. He is eager to succeed. He needs to be able to tell future employers that he'd achieved something. This was his first commission; he would make sure he'd done it to the best of his ability. He settled back in his seat and soon the plane was airborne. Thinking about Mr. Baker who said he'd telephone about 1930 hours to tie up any loose ends, but never did. He wondered if he was acting efficiently, upon his own initiative. He kept saying to himself that he was doing his very best. He released his seat belt and relaxed.

Clearance of the German airport was quick and thorough; soon he was outside seeking a taxi. A young man was waving a notice board above his head with the name Mr. Brandon. At a gesture of Vic's hand the man approached and said he was to take him to the district court, and directed him to a waiting car.

"I am Mark Jansen, to assist you all the time as you need" he said in good understandable English.

"I knew this place well" he added as the car manoeuvres through the street. He is impressed by the rate of recovery from war damage to the new modern designs of buildings constructed over the years since he was last in Dusseldorf. He was familiar with this town in his army days, but now recognises only a few landmarks. It could be another place entirely. Almost before he realised it, the car stops outside the court building; his destination point. Mark escorts his charge to court number 4, and leaves him with the court clerk.

"I'll put the car in the official parking place and await your return" he said, and departed holding the door open for a woman with a striking official appearance. She enters the court; moving close by Vic and passing, she takes a public seat in the front row, directly under the bench. Vic thought her to be the court recorder, or perhaps from the local press suddenly the court's in session....

He was pleased to find the court personnel to be helpful and understanding of his predicament. He was invited to address the court in the English language on behalf of Mr. Baker. The penalty, fine and costs set by the court were paid, the documents stamped and issued releasing the estate car into his custody. He was also to go to the police vehicle compound to pay the recovery cost and other charges before being allowed to drive the car away.

Vic standing, thanked the court, and turned taking a few paces to leave and almost bumped into a woman standing behind him.

"I'm sorry," he said politely, and caught the fragrance of her perfume.

"No, it's my mistake, I didn't realise you were going to move so suddenly. I am sorry" she said smiling, and their eyes met momentarily in pleasant acknowledgement of each other. She turned and walked away leaving him staring as she gracefully strolled across the court floor to another exit. She turned to glance in his direction, and left the building. He'd thought her to be German, but she spoke perfect English. She had listened to the whole case proceedings and took notes.

The clerk to the court put the necessary documents into his hand and explained how to release the car from the police compound. Vic was only half listening, his mind still upon the woman, somehow something struck him about her. He could not say what it was; only that it hit him.

"Who was that woman? She's just leaving over there" he asked the clerk, as their eyes looked in that direction, the door closing behind her.

"I don't know, this is an open court, people come in at any time. I haven't seen her here before".

Thanking the clerk, he leaves with his documents and is met upon the court entrance steps by Mark, who is aware that the next stop is the police presidium to arrange handover of the car. As they are ready to leave the parking lot and moving towards the exit, a white Mercedes car passes in front, driven by the same lady that attended the court. She turns her head in acknowledgment, and drives on ahead. Her car soon moves into traffic and out of sight, but Vic catches a glimpse of its rear number plate with a British registration number displayed.

Mark manoeuvres his car with skill and agility through the town roads and streets, soon to stop outside the police headquarters. As his passenger gets out, he is advised to take all relevant documents inside with him. Mark then said he would await further instructions.

At the top of the entrance steps waiting to greet Vic Brandon, was a tall, smartly dressed police sergeant. He offers his hand.

"I am Sergeant Mann, I am instructed to help you in any way I can" he said with confidence, as if to let Vic know that he was in charge of proceedings at this particular constabulary. The building was quiet and peaceful for a police station. They walked a long corridor, the end of which was a canteen for the use of the station staff. They sat together at a table and chatted whilst lunch was ordered and prepared.

"The work shop have put the battery on charge which will take about an hour, so I thought it suitable to have lunch in the meantime".

"Thank you". Also expecting that the car would be checked over at the same time. Vic had not seen the car, and asked about the accident damage. The sergeant said that it had been attended to sufficiently, making it road worthy for night driving, and there will be moderate costs.

Over lunch they completed formalities and carried on a conversation. It was noticeable that the sergeant was eager to exercise his command of the English language and mostly carried the topics forward. Underneath his official attitude, he was a nice person, with a pleasant personality, doing a difficult job. He was well built, well groomed, and a little arrogant. The type some women liked. They enjoyed their lunch, and each others company. Whilst still chatting, they left the table, and walked to the exit stairs, down towards the motor pool at the back of the police station.

Seeing the car for the first time Vic was surprised its only a little damaged, and that it's a top of the range model. The estate car had been checked over, and the engine running smoothly. The fuel gauge showed sufficient fuel for the journey, and the near side headlamp damage was temporarily repaired and working. Standing by, and apparently being helpful, was Mark Janson, who asked if he would be further required, but was dismissed by Sergeant Mann, saying that he would escort the car through the town traffic en route to Ostend. Mark left after signing his instruction note, signing him off.

"I will lead ahead in a police car, and you follow closely behind. It's about five kilometres" said the sergeant.

Soon both cars were weaving their way through the town streets and roads as normal traffic. It's a heavy car Vic thought. The type he had never previously driven, but immediately got the feel of it, and liked it. He felt good about being in possession; it was the prime part of his consignment, and now he's on the way to fulfilment.

It was a few minutes past four when the motorway came into sight and the police escort waved goodbye, in doing so directed the car and driver on ahead. Vic had travelled this motorway route many times in the years past, each time in a military vehicle, which often took much longer because of road repair work to war damaged surfaces and bridges. One-way traffic and diversions were many then. Now the way is clear, the roads and bridges have long since been repaired, and he is estimating his time of arrival at the ferry dock at Ostend about 2130 hours. The weather is fine, with a clear late summer sky, and the going is good with light to moderate traffic. He settles comfortably into the driver's seat, there's no hurry so he takes things easy, driving carefully whilst many cars overtake, speeding on ahead. A white Mercedes car passes, which causes his mind to recall the white Mercedes car with the English registration number plate leaving the court car park, driven by the woman who spoke a few English words to him in the county court. He remembers her voice, polite, gentle and with a slight American accent as if she had previously lived in America. She was a fair brunette with sparkling grey/green eyes spaced symmetrically apart enhancing her mature face. As she spoke her smile revealed a set of pearly white teeth set behind her soft lips. That's what hit him, her smile and her eyes, it was only momentary but it embellished itself upon his mind.

He had met many women of different nationalities in his soldiering career but he cannot recall any one of them that struck him so profoundly upon so brief an encounter. He sees her leaving the court turning gracefully and correctly walking away revealing her correctly curved figure and leaving him standing bewildered before the bench.

A car horn sounds, which brought his attention back to the road along which he's driving. He realises that meeting her ever so briefly, has not only stuck in his mind but she has also developed in his mind. (She wore little facial make-up, neatly conservatively dressed in a two-piece costume, lovely long legs in high heel shoes. It all adds up to one thing, she is an attractive woman). Who is she? Why did she attend the court? How will he get answers? He asked himself. It suddenly occurred to him that she might be the car owner's girlfriend. Perhaps Thomas Baker's fiancé. He being in America and unable to attend himself, she keenly listened to the court proceedings and perhaps, attended the police headquarters after. He thought it no coincident that an English speaking woman should be in the court at that time.

If she had interest in the case she could have paid the court dues and cost. Thereby retrieving the car herself. No, that doesn't seem to be logical, he thought. Perhaps a freelance reporter but dismissed that immediately. His mind still dwelt upon this mystery woman as he drove on into the evening. His eye catches a road sign advising that the Niederland Border was ahead and that everything including passports must be shown. The Border control personnel checked every document, the car and his passport before allowing him to proceed. His ego raises a little as he thinks about driving such a smart car, the opportunity never arose before and he was going to make the most of it. He enters the car with some importance and dignity as if they had been together for years and the car silently moves away. As the car enters the mainstream of motorway traffic, other cars are dashing by some with headlights shining. It will be dark before he's passed the Belgium frontier and another hour to enter the ferry dock at Ostend, on route to England...

A few military lorries passed in the opposite road lane, young soldiers of the occupation Army in Europe. Shapes, Images, memories, colours and patterns flash through his mind. The early days as a young soldier … the oath of allegiance … the fear they would ask his age because he had stated that he was a year older than he was. Learning to stumble

18

about in the blackout … his first training sergeant … equipment chucked at him from the back of a truck… the bloody ill-fitting uniform, boots, too big and stiff leather … a palliasse he stuffed with straw. Three new blankets, impregnated with antiseptic, … the barber scalping his head like a shorn sheep … the jabs with bent blunt needles … eternal square bashing … route marches … assault courses … reveille at 0600 hours in bleak winter … your bed turned up if you don't stand … shaving in cold water. The incessant, cleaning and polishing … if it moves salute it … if it don't, paint it. Spud bashing with penknife … pot and pan cleaning … long queues for food, dolloped into your cold mess tins, the ever bad jokes and bad language, rumours about girls, and continuing barrack room bragging about sex. The persistent harsh discipline: learning to kill with a rifle and bayonet, machine gun, hand grenade and learning to kill, kill the enemy … being expendable… stripped naked standing in the cold for medical examination, vaccinated and every hole in your body probed. That's all history now. He must have been mad to have suffered it "It's all for your own good" they said.

The images stopped as he read the road sign pointing to the ferry port 15 kms. He's nothing to do with the military now. He is a civilian on his first assignment and determined to make a success of it. He's feeling proud of himself driving a posh car into the marshalling area and lining up with other vehicles scheduled to board the ferry to Dover, slowly he looked around to take note of the directional signs. He was in the right queue. With more than 50 cars in front. If it takes only two minutes to load each car he reckoned it would be about an hour and a half before sailing and then the voyage to Dover about three and a half hours. He switches on the interior light to read the car ferry booking document previously arranged and paid for by his sponsor. Yes, all is in order and he's well within time. Mr. Baker said that he would arrange everything and so far he's done a good job, but he didn't phone as he said he would to tie up loose ends. Perhaps something came up to direct his attention elsewhere. Vic had got used to that in the past everything arranged: "Here are your marching orders, railway warrant, ration card and letter of introduction to you new unit's officer Commanding. You will be taken to the local railway station by army truck leaving 0800 hours tomorrow.

The Lesser Evil

Have all your kit ready and book out immediately before going'. No word of 'do you mind' 'is that alright with you?" no politeness is considered nor expected, orders are orders, do it, don't say goodbye or thank you. That's the army code – no time for courtesies or sympathies get on with it!

He stops himself, he's trying to put all that behind him but it still lingers in his mind. Often he has flash backs to traumatic shock situations. Suddenly he was sitting bolt upright with terror gripping him. The noise paralysed him and tore through his body and set his nerves on edge. He'd heard it before dangerously close; he managed to look out, with a start. The car horn behind, was screaming like bombs raining down. The cars in front were moving forwards in a column. Quickly he drives to catch up in the queue and within a few minutes the car is secured aboard the ship bound for Dover. He is relieved and safe.

Now is the time to relax with a glass of beer, which he buys from the lounge bar and saunters to find a place to sit. A party of lorry drivers noticing his situation move around the table to make room for him "Oy here mate, I'm sure you can get your rump in here," one man said. The other five men smiling and nodding in agreement they bid him welcome as they would any other heavy goods vehicle driver on long continental journeys. They seem to recognise each other instinctively. They chatted together friendly, often bragging about their various escapades abroad, they would each bring in contraband in small amounts on nearly every trip, this was perks, but never narcotics or hard drugs. The customs officials are very strict about bringing in hard stuff, but would overlook moderate amounts of wines, spirits and tobaccos, One of the older men related how a driver brought in a container with a false floor under which was found over one million pounds sterling, street market, value of hard drugs and being in possession, he is currently serving 10 years in prison. The custom boys are aware of every trick and dodge, a spare wheel was found packed full of drugs, fuel tanks with false bottoms, and they know every trick in the book. We have our photos taken every time we go out, and again upon return. Studying tacho-graph records shows every journey, time and distance covered. They expect, and get cooperation, that's why they don't mind if we bring in petty things. Its big hauls they're looking for, and the international gangs behind it all. Smuggling is big business with big rewards and bigger penalties. A few of them were well versed in this haulage business and had seen it all before, they knew the score.

"What ya driving mate?" he looked at Vic with curiosity in his voice. Lorry drivers were often asking each other about the reliability, make and type of other heavy goods vehicles they were driving, it's a matter of professional pride and perhaps a little jealously.

Vic replies, "A Volvo, I think," not being aware that the Volvo factory produced one of the better-known reliable intercontinental heavy haulage trucks, and before he said another word he was in the league with them, he was immediately accepted as one of the truckers. Why should he bother to explain that he drove an estate car, not a truck? The man doing all the talking decides "its time we had another beer". Vic stood up assuming himself in clique with them and said "I'll get them in", he looks at each of them in turn for their choice and soon returns from the bar with a tray of seven pints, which he puts upon the table, takes one himself, and raises his glass saying "cheers" looking at each man, and smiling they are all given friendly responses to his gesture, and all drinking at Mister Baker's expense.

Looking over his glass of beer, his eyes focus, in the distance across the lounge he catches a glimpse of the woman he saw in the Dusseldorf court, he stared across the spacious lounge above many passengers relaxing and dozing in the soft furniture. She was walking towards an exit. He recognised the way she moved, distinctive with charm and poise. He was sure it must be her; he was determined to find out. Putting his glass down upon the low table, he rushes weaving his way between reclining passengers and the furniture, to the door through which she left the saloon. The door opened onto the portside promenade deck. The night air and cold sea breeze hit him; suddenly his mind is crystal clear and sharp. He looked both ways along the deck so far as the dim lighting would allow, but no person was in sight. Bewildered he could not imagine where she could have gone in such a short time. He stood silently looking into the night air thinking perhaps he was mistaken. Why should he care? Their eyes had met for a moment about 12 hours ago, she seemed to be curious about him and that impacted his mind and disturbed him. Is she aboard this ship bound for Dover or is it wishful thinking or is he hallucinating? He hadn't drunk so much beer but he could be tired. He settled down on a sofa and slept for two hours. He is awakened with a start by a voice coming over the public address system, advising passengers that the ship will be docking in fifteen minutes. All are now getting their luggage together making ready to leave; there will be no time to get a cup of tea, which he would have loved at that lonely hour.

The cars in front are moving slowly, disembarking, getting onto the dock. Ahead are immigration and custom control barriers, through which he must go with the car he is bringing into the country.

The first controller saw only his passport and his face, without comment. Moving on to declare that he was returning a UK registered Volvo estate car, he placed all relevant documents into the hand of the customs officer, a serious looking man, middle age, with naval rank type insignia upon the lower sleeves of his uniform.

"Do you own this car sir?"

"No, you will see with the documents, I passed to you a letter from the owner Mr. Thomas Baker, authorising me to collect the car from the police compound in Dusseldorf Germany after it had been released by the court. I'm only the driver, but I'd love to own such a car".

"Thank you sir". The officer continues to study each document in detail.

"Is this the court release document printed in German?" he asked.

"Yes, it bears the car registration number, description and the courts office seal stamp, with the magistrate's signature".

"This is another German document, what is this one for?"

Seemingly the officer cannot read German, which is surprising.

"You can see that it's issued by the headquarters of the Nord Rhein district police. It gives over to me the custody of the car after certain costs have been paid, and with it is a receipt of payment".

"Thank you sir" he nodded.

"Do you also have insurance cover for this car sir?"

"Yes, it's with the other papers in your hand". He takes his time to look at each carefully and asks,

"May I see your passport for identification?"

He returns the passport without comment, but looks at its owner suspiciously, studying his face.

"Thank you sir, please open the car rear door" he requested in such sincere manner, that it was becoming apparent that this car was not going any further until every detail was satisfactorily covered. The customs had to look for cars being imported without paying UK import duty and or tax. The interior was quickly checked, and the officer walked around it and said,

"I will take your papers into the office to be cleared, it will take a few minutes".

Waiting seemed a long time; all the other cars had gone on their way. It's past 0230 hours before the customs officer returned with all the documents, each duly stamped with official clearance.

"Thank you sir, all is in order, sorry to have delayed you". Then he said in German "Have a good journey home".

Vic smiled. "Thanks, goodbye" and proceeded upon the last leg of his consignment journey. The thought gave him a considerable smug feeling of achievement. The roads from the town of Dover were quiet at the early hour, and soon he was speeding along the main highway to Southampton. Only a few cars travelled the same route, most of them overtaking as he slowed down to read a roadway sign, 'Service area 5 miles' which meant a refreshing cup of tea or coffee, and something to eat. Passing the sign a white Mercedes appeared within his headlamp beam for a few seconds. Could that be the same car he noticed in Germany the previous day? He couldn't see who was driving it in the night. Perhaps by shear coincidence it could be the mystery woman he thought he saw aboard the ship. His thirst directed his attention to the 'pull in' sign, and within a few minutes the car was parked within about 20 paces of the café entrance.

There were more lorries than cars, that made the choice in parking easy, many car parking places were vacant. Entering the café he saw the place was busy. Lorry drivers prefer driving at night when the roads are not heavily congested. They take rest breaks in such places that earn a reputation for serving good food at any time. He got himself a welcome cup of tea and a big sausage and bacon sandwich. Sitting at the table, enjoying his breakfast, he picks up the previous days newspaper. The headlines 'Customs clamp down on drugs'. The article goes on to explain that gangs are getting desperate; the street market price is rising, and there has been fighting in the nightclubs.

Reading this he reflects upon what he had heard from the lorry driver a few hours ago aboard the ship and that he thought he saw that attractive woman again in the distance across the ships lounge. Why should she linger in his mind? He has known many young women, few dwelled long after first acquaintance. He shrugs off the thought, reminding himself that he was on the home run that in about two hours he could be entering the car park in Southampton, mission accomplished.

Walking out into the early morning fresh air, he breathes deeply seeing there is a glimmer of daylight upon the eastern horizon. He walks towards the car, finding the key in his pocket; he places it to open the car door. He is aware of a person behind, he turns to see, his head is struck a vicious glancing blow with a heavy dull object. Half conscious he staggers and falls to his knees. Amidst the bells and rattle sounds in his head he hears the words,

"Get the key, the bloody key". A hand is wrenching at his key chain. The key is in his hand. The other end of the chain is secured to his waist belt. Instinctively his army training kicks in. He twists and turns towards his assailant, and in the same instant recovering his stance, he drives the point of his right elbow with full force into his attacker's throat. He pivots continues to bring his left fist with great force into his stomach, forcing the wind and vomit up his gullet to fill his mouth whilst he choked and reeled with pain. Another onslaught immediately follows from another person with a cosh. This time the blow fell upon his right shoulder, he saw it coming, twisted and avoided its full effect, but a severe pain shot down his arm. There are no rules in unarmed combat. Instantly Vic turned to the other assailant, grabbing the weapon with his left hand, and swiftly jerks his knee into the man's testicles, with sufficient force to lift him off the ground. With a head-but, Vic drives him backwards and shoves him into his mate, who unsteadily stands recovering from his ordeal, only to be thrown down again. Before both men could think of further action, and whilst they are squirming with pain, Vic quickly enters the car.

24

V J Tarry

The rear wheels spin, sending up dust, as he speedily drives away out of the car park, to enter the roadway again. Suffering more pain from his shoulder than the bump upon his head, he mentally checks himself over to conclude that there's no serious damage. Charged with nervous anxiety, and driving wildly, he is eager to get as far as possible away from the assailants who might at this moment be chasing after him. Why? He asks himself, why did two men attack him? Was it their intention to steal the car? Post war cars fetched good prices. No, perhaps it was himself they wanted? He needed time and quiet to think and nurse his wounds. The next exit, he drives out of the roadway onto another road, and again changed to a secondary road which led him to a small village.

He found a car park space by a river and stopped. He was sure that if anybody followed, he would have lost them now. The riverside was peaceful and quiet, the morning sunrise made everything bright, green and clear. A few people were beginning to attend to their daily routine in the village street. A man walked across the car park to open the public toilet, an opportunity to bathe his head wound, and freshen up. A bump the size of a small golf ball was covered mostly by his thick black hair. His shoulder pain and bruising he exercised as he returned to the car. Before entering, he walks around the car looking at it with interest and curiosity. He opens the hatch, and studies the interior, examines the spare wheel, there's nothing unusual. Opening the rear doors he glances around the inside, lifts the seats, and finds everything new and undisturbed. He opens up the engine bonnet, staring inside sees nothing amiss.

Perplexed, he feels the hurt of his head bump, and wonders why was he so brutally attacked? He had heard a man say 'get the key', they must therefore want the car, there must be something in or about this car that made it worth while, and they know something. Mr Baker, who commissioned him to get the car, arranged everything and paid in advance, would not likely try and steal it. No, somebody else wants it, or wants something from it. He is sure the car must have been followed from Dover. The two attackers must have had full description of it, and waited for it to appear from the dock. Driving off the road into the service area for refreshment gave an opportunity and facility to both men to perpetrate their intended crime. Pondering recent past events, he feels sure it's the car they want, although he hasn't seen it, there must be something of considerable value hidden within the bodywork, perhaps underneath.

Across the road he had noticed a garage as he drove into the village. Intending to see the underneath of the car, he asked the proprietor to put it upon a car hoist and allow him to inspect it.

"This car's in good condition, there's nothing loose or missing, everything's fine" the mechanic said. Then his eyes moved to the front bumper, closely he examined it, turned and moved to examine the rear bumper from underneath.

"I've never seen that before, they are both boxed in, making them more substantial, giving extra strength" he said.

"Why would that be, are the bumpers not made that way by the factory?"

"No, the front and rear are normally steel, and then covered with a plastic open section to the front and the same to the rear. The plastic improves the appearance and styling. Most modern cars use plastic nowadays". He looked with curiosity towards the customer asking,

"Do you own this car sir?" he didn't answer that question.

"How would anybody make up such a box section, say in a workshop such as yours?" Vic asked.

"Well, we've never done it here, but its explained in detail in the trade journals. It's what they called plastic welding technique using controlled hot gas. Accident damaged cars are often repaired using the plastic welding process" he said.

"The box bumper bars – can they be removed?"

"Look here, if you remove the four bolts, that's two each side, the complete thing will just fall off. There's one other thing, I've noticed it's a front wheel drive! I'm not sure, but I don't think Volvo made a front drive car, but this is one so I could be wrong".

"Anything else interesting you notice?" asked Vic.

"Not underneath. The front nearside has had a bang at sometime, and has been bodged up, perhaps to make it usable for the moment. You should do something about that". Before the mechanic could say anything further, he thanked him and paid what he asked for the service and returned to the riverside car park.

The Lesser Evil

REVELATIONS

Vic Brandon's curiosity is aroused; the boxed sections of the front and rear bumpers have been made up for a particular purpose. He's determined to explore further, using a pen knife blade he finds a weak spot in the plastic, and starts to make a hole. He would not do this in the garage because the mechanic expressed a curiosity not to be encouraged. After a few minutes a small hole appeared in the plastic, working the blade deeper until a hole big enough to take a pencil was made. The knife blade with flat uppermost carried a white powder like substance upon it. He had seen this stuff before in Egypt during Suez campaign. It's cocaine and the car's back and front bumpers are loaded with the stuff. The thought of the dramatic find disturbed his mind. Whilst he chewed up some paper and plugged the hole blood coursed through his veins and his heart beats faster. A quick calculation: the length of the bumper 66 inches x closed section 9 inches x projected part about 10.5 inches adds up to 6237 cubic inches in the front and about the same in the rear. 12500 cubic inches together, that's a lot of drug space in the car. He realises that he has been duped into a scheme to bring this evil stuff into the country, who will believe he didn't know about it? He's guilty.

Vic's shocked and at the same time exhilarated at the thought, like the drug itself makes him feel like a dangerous fool. His brain is running away with him – stop! Logic enters his head. This matter is serious, decidedly serious and needs proper appraisal; he'll have to do it himself.

The Lesser Evil

Hysterically he laughs remembering he gave his address and telephone number in his advertisement. Mr Baker who gave him this job must know exactly what is stowed secretly within the car. Baker will be expecting to see the vehicle arriving at the Southampton airport car park. The two thugs who coshed him attempting to steal the car must also know what was in it. He begins to see what a stupid naïve fool he has been, disciplined and eager to do his duty without question, his military training made him gullible. Baker must have seen that in the advertisement and in subsequent discussions about duties he was willing to perform.

Thinking clearer now the cosh on his head might have knocked better sense into him although it hurt like hell. The two men attacking him were not young, fit nor agile. In the dim morning light he distinguished no features but the words 'the key, get the bloody key' were spoken in a Scottish accent. Nobody could have realised that he would drive into that particular service area it was a decision he made instantly he saw the road sign. He was therefore followed from Dover and the intended hijackers must have a full description of the car, its contents and estimated time of arrival from the continent. They were lying in waiting for the car. He has no idea of the street market value of the drugs in the car and supposed it to be a great amount. At least three people seem to have a better idea of the cargo value; he's sitting on a fortune and expected to deliver it to Southampton.

Thinking that he should be completing the contract by delivering the car to the airport car park in Southampton soon and surely somebody will be waiting to take it from him; he can hear the person saying, 'thanks mate you've done a good job. I'll take over now'. That would be the end of the matter. He was foolish to have got tricked into this racket and got beaten-up into the bargain. If the goods are not delivered as expected somebody's going to be knocking on his door and it won't be a social call.

He sees himself guilty of bringing illegal drugs into the country and of being in possession. He would have difficulty explaining that to a court. The thought caused his mind to reflect upon the fact that the police in Germany held this car for some weeks before releasing it to his charge. They had time and opportunity to examine it and it's reasonable

28

to suppose that the police discovered the drugs intended for somebody in England. The British customs would be alerted and the car put under surveillance expecting somebody to eventually come to collect it. He remembers the customs officer at Dover examined the various papers but didn't take so much care about the car, it was delayed whilst documents were stamped. Somebody in Germany cleverly made up the cunning boxing arrangement of the front and rear bumpers and other parts filling each with cocaine before sealing. Then the car passes through Dover enroute to its intended destination. At the Southampton car park handing over of the car to an accomplice, the police step in to arrest both the recipient and himself, he's the scapegoat caught with the drugs red-handed.

He's sure that this consignment of drugs if having been discovered would be used as a bait to get to the international organisers behind the drug smuggling racket. Two other men tried unsuccessfully to take the car and inadvertently changed the intended course of events. Now he decides that he is not going to hand over this treasure to anyone at the proposed rendezvous. He never liked the use of drugs, illegal or otherwise, they never appealed to him, and he wasn't promoting any evil drug trade either. An inspiration struck him. He's the only person in the world who knows where the car is.

It flashed across his mind that the car could be bugged, sending out signals to make it traceable. He starts looking into every conceivable place for a signal device and almost dismantles the interior and found nothing. Of course the intention would be to have the car followed and the woman in the white Mercedes might be with the crooks who attacked him or perhaps police or customs. Her car might have a mobile radio phone in it reporting every significant movement to anybody. She could have been in the service area car park when he was fighting off the attackers. His speedy exit successful in not being followed by anyone put the estate car out of reach of interested parties … He alone can contact anybody he wishes upon his own terms when he's inclined to do so.

His head is throbbing less now that his mind is on the road driving towards his resident destination. He's avoiding all main roads and travelling along byways and secondary roads, he's aware a multi storey car park had been built in Bournemouth. Parking in such a place gives car security for a small fee per 24 hour stay.

It's more than two hours later when he parks the car unobtrusively, puts coins into the slot machine and obtains a ticket. It's only a short walking distance to the bus stop and takes a short bus journey to his flat to wait events. A state of anxiety comes over him, somebody will be phoning or arriving at his door demanding to know where the car is, they may have realised that he discovered its value and is holding out for more money.

He takes a quick shower to freshen up, eases his aches, pains and clears his head. Frequently he looks out of the window overseeing the rear of the building in which there are many bachelor flats such as he is renting. He is keen to see if any cars arrive with dubious characters. Turning away to make himself a late breakfast with coffee, he sets out to plot his next move. He has a car full of drugs, a great bargaining factor and he puzzles how to start the dealing. The men who attacked him wanted to take the car by force. Who were they? Even if he knew them he vows never to make contact. He feels sure that soon Baker will be demanding explanations with menaces. The police in Germany and England must be aware and likewise the customs. Either could be making contact with him soon upon no uncertain terms.

He sits quietly thinking, like the calm before the storm! How is he to get the best advantage out of any situation that may arise, should he make contact with the authorities? It will look better for him if he is able and willing to cooperate. No, he sees little hope in cooperation, 'Thank you very much for your help' and 'much of your work was appreciated'. He's known it all before, others getting praise while he gets pittance or jail. This time he has the upper hand; he's going to get the rewards and praises. Moving to get another cup of coffee, the telephone rings. 'This is it, he said aloud. He was ready to start dealing with Mr Baker who no doubt will be enraged. He will tell him that he was tricked into the contract to bring in the car and now everything has changed because he knows its worth. He will only surrender the car after negotiating a much better deal. Lifting the hand set to his ear he casually said:

"Hello, Vic here" in a matter of fact sort of way. An unfamiliar voice asked

"Are you Mister Victor Brandon?"

"Yes that's me"

"I am Mister John Hardwick H.M Customs and Excise in Poole, I must speak with you urgently", Oh, that sets his mind racing they must know.

"Why?"

"We have good reason to believe that you brought an estate car into England from Germany this morning and it is vital that we meet to discuss the implications of your actions".

He's stunned; his brain is rushing madly about going over events of the last 2 days. He knows, of course at Dover all the documents were taken away for examination in which would be in his name, address and phone number. What does this caller want to discuss so urgently he must find out if he knows about the drugs?

"Mr Hardwick can you identify your self further and better?"

"I will be pleased to do that if you will meet me for lunch in half an hour at Jock Gordon's restaurant by the quay in Poole, taxi drivers will know where it is. In the mean time leave your phone off the hook so that nobody can contact you and speak to nobody before meeting me. I must impress upon you the urgency of our meeting".

"How will I know you in the restaurant?"

"Ask the waiter, he will direct you to me at a reserved table discreetly placed, we will talk uninterrupted".

In the taxi he's worried, customs officers are not in the habit of buying lunch for anybody unless they want something. They know he has the car but don't know where it is, otherwise they could arrest him and seize the car. There's something else, he is eager to find out the urgency of this lunchtime meeting. He can sense it, there's a deal in the offering, something's up but he cannot figure it yet.

"This way Mr Brandon sir" said the waiter pointing to a quiet corner, he leads on ahead. A man stands up from his chair. He's tall, about 50; well-groomed ex-navel officer type offering his hand he said:

The Lesser Evil

"Thanks for coming so promptly". His handshake was firm, felt genuine in which one could have confidence.

"John Hardwick" he smiled pleasantly.

"Will you have a drink before we eat?"

"Thank you, brandy and dry ginger please"

"I'll have whisky and water" he said to the waiter, who passed each of them a menu.

"Mr Brandon you may have guessed that this is a business meeting of considerable urgency and importance. I must formally introduce myself. I am Mister John Hardwick. I am a senior customs and excise officer of the narcotics intelligence investigation department. I will make notes of this meeting for a further report. I am to warn you that anything you say will be noted and maybe used as evidence in subsequent action. Before proceeding further it is a requirement that at any interview of this nature another person is to be present to corroborate words spoken to you and by you. The report I make will be countersigned by the other person, my assistant college who will be along soon," he said in a matter of fact way. Vic is familiar with the official jargon and attitude, he never thought to meet it in civil life and he has no liking for it. This must mean that the customs are thinking of charging him with something, perhaps smuggling amongst other things.

"Its just routine procedures that we have to go through, you understand!" lifting his glass he said, "They serve an excellent steak here".

Whilst enjoying the meal Vic was asked about his army life in a compromising way: he had served for many years and showed reluctance to discuss his life in the army and tried to change the subject to the navy life of his inquisitor. They had been lunching for nearly an hour and no mention of the urgency of the meeting. No mention of the car or drugs. The waiting causing anxiety like waiting for a trial, perhaps he should surrender the car to Mr Hardwick there and then and tell Mr Baker that the customs officials at Dover have seized the car. The thought vanished in a flash, Hardwick promptly stood up.

"This is my college, Jenny Robins" he said, turning quickly to introduce her. Vic, taking her hand a state of bewilderment overcame him, he was dumbfounded, he'd never expected to meet her here; his minds in

32

a turmoil she smiled saying "I'm so sorry to be late". The same attractive woman he'd briefly met the previous day in the Dusseldorf court. Bewilderment gradually changed to pleasant surprise as again their eyes met, she smiled pleasantly excusing everything. Now he knows she's a customs officer he's shocked, and can't release her hand. She pulls away. She had had lunch before arriving and the two of them were now eager to get down to the purpose of the meeting. Documents were produced, they both looked at him seriously, sitting opposite he's waiting for the opening words. Mr Hardwick places a particular paper upon the table.

"You are Victor John Brandon! It states that upon this document with your address etc. It is the official secrets act statement form, you will be required to sign it before we can proceed any further". He looks at it with deep concern; it had previously been typed out with correct details. The very formal, efficient procedural attitude of his attendance put his mind into a state of flux wondering what next will happen, what else do they know about him.

"I've signed one of these things about four months ago, the day I left the army I don't need to read it. I know what it is all about".

"That may be, Mr. Brandon but for this occasion you'll have to sign this one" he said, pushing the form closer to him and putting a wet ink pen upon the table. Hesitating he picks up the instrument and puts his full signature to the document and shoves it and the pen back. Jenny looked at him and smiled and said "Thank you" as if he had done something to please her. John Hardwick put the document in his briefcase and said

"Now down to business" with his masterful official voice, he leads on to say

"Mr Brandon we have good reason to believe that in the early hours of Thursday morning you brought into England via Dover a car carrying a substantial amount of illegal drugs without declaring the drugs to her majesty's customs and excise at Dover. Further you remain in illegal possession of the same drugs and that you are acting as an agent for another person in dealing with illegal drugs". Listening to each word he realised that his best bet would be to declare his hand and officially surrender the car. Jenny looked straight at him shaking her head as if she was reading his mind, her eyes were saying.

The Lesser Evil

"Don't do it!" he nods in understanding. John Hardwick looked up from his writing.

"Do you fully understand the implication of what I have told you?"

"Yes, I think I understand your words"

"Very well then, I now need to explain the position to you further. There are people serving prison terms for having done the same as you, each of them pleaded not guilty and offered the court mitigating circumstances. One name appears in at least two of these court cases Reginald Alexander Baker". He said. The name makes Vic's ears prick up as it coursed through his brain he'd know that name to his detriment now.

"It is this man Baker we believe is behind a very big drug smuggling racket, we believe he set up the scheme to modify the car you drove to bring drugs into England, drugs hidden in obscure compartments. He then waited an opportunity to find some eager naïve person to bring the car into this country". They both stared at Vic. He knew what that meant, he's embarrassed and said nothing, and how could he know the mind of crooks and smugglers. The police in Dusseldorf take into their vehicle compound many cars, some stolen, accident damaged and or abandoned. Each is checked for identification and the last known owner informed about police cost, recovery and court proceedings. If there is no action within six months the vehicle is sold. During the course of vehicle movement within the police compound the estate car sustains slight damage to the rear, cracking the encased plastic bumper bar, exposing the drug cocaine. The car displayed an English registration number. The owner, in answer to previous correspondence, was planning to send somebody to collect and drive the car back to England. Immediately the police in Germany informed the British customs through the highest echelons of their departments. British customs excepted responsibility for a ruse to allow the car to enter England in the normal way and trace its movements to its recipient, where upon the police would be poised to pounce and arrest all persons directly concerned in the matter whilst taking possession of the contraband car.

Vic Brandon lifts his hand to touch his wounded head; the bump still large had healed slightly but was still painful. Jenny Robins notices his movement, came round the table to help. She looked at the inflamed bulge

34

gently and sympathetically, touched it hurting him a little but he didn't flinch. She realised that he'd sustained painful injury and gave him two aspirin tablets.

"I'm sorry," she said. He saw in her eyes that she meant it. He nodded thanks and felt a little better for her sympathy.

"I think now we should tell you that Jenny Robin here was assigned to the case very soon after we arranged with the German police and the court in Dusseldorf to release the car to a named person. You now know that Jenny was in that court, she was to see that man face to face for future identification purposes and from there on to discreetly follow him and record his movements with the special drug laden car. She was also in attendance at the service area car park when you were attacked".

Vic looked at her seeing the picture clearly now he was about to say something. She spoke first. Jenny Robin, referring to her diary, recording his movements aboard the ferryboat and to the customs checkout at Dover. She was present in their Dover office when all the documents were photocopied and returned. He was delayed a little with formalities whilst she prepared to follow the car to its destination. The car was seen driven into the service area. She followed, parked her car between lorries to be inconspicuous, and sat waiting. It was a good vantage point she observed the two men attacking him and she moved with other bystanders to help. The action was over so erratically the car speeding away fiercely that she saw very little but she did see one of the assailants clearly as he lifted his body reeling from the pain in his groin.

Her diary records showed that she speedily drove out onto the road in pursuit of the estate car but never sighted it.

"The attack was an unfortunate occurrence, it utterly destroyed our plans, however not all is lost, the man I saw is known to us, as Ken Flowers and his business partner associate we believe to be Benny Wheeler. These two men are in fierce competition with Reg Baker and his partner in crime Brian Boothe" she said, appearing full of confidence!'

"The two men you encountered and dealt with so effectively intended to snatch the car from you. How they would know its value is a mystery at this stage in our proceedings".

"How did they know about its arrival into England, date and time?" he asked John Hardwick.

"We can not answer that just now but we suspect that they have intelligence connections that might lead into our organisation or perhaps they simply read your advertisement putting 2 and 2 together. Never underestimate the criminal mind, the stakes are high these men are cunning, clever and ruthless".

"Do I understand that within your office, customs organisation somebody is passing information to the men who beat me up?"

"You could be right, as yet we have only suspicions, that's why we are here meeting in this restaurant" he looks around, the place is nearly empty, one man only sat a few tables away.

"This meeting is incognito, we don't want you to be seen in our offices at any time. You must understand that you are important to us, we want Baker but for the time being we have you and you have the car into which is secreted about 2 million pounds worth at street market value cocaine. The original intent was for you to deliver the car full of drugs and that's what you are going to do". Jenny looked at him seriously nodding with agreement with the words and said

"The German police force found many cleverly concealed compartments in the car, more then you might imagine the car was redesigned to receive as much cocaine as possible without changing its outwards appearance. The police breaking into the various compartments would also mean resealing them and the police didn't have time nor the expertise therefore the car continues as intended, it was last seen driven by you". In an awkward pause Vic smiled and said.

"After escaping my attackers I drove the car to a quiet place to recollect my thoughts and examine the car. Realising there must be something valuable stowed within the car, I probed and found a substance like cocaine. The car is now secured in a multi storey car park about 2 miles away and I'd like to be rid of it!"

Hardwick's face was very stern, his eyes cunning like a fox looked at Jenny and Vic... and said

"Well we will have to devise a plan to get the cargo of drugs into the hands of Mr Baker and be poised with police support to arrest him immediately he takes possession"

"No" Jenny said 'He will never expose himself in such a way; it will never be that simple. I've had a chance to study some of this mans tactics, he will always get somebody else to do the dirty work'. She turned to look at Vic, he knew what that meant and he'd no liking for the implication.

"Have you ever seen the man Baker, the man who sent you on this errand?" It was a rhetorical question Vic just shook his head and she said, No.

"The car should have been delivered to Southampton rendezvous about five hours ago. Do I understand it was to be left where Vic had parked his car? Somebody will see that transaction and when deemed safe to do so will drive away the goods, job done, no faces seen. Isn't that their plan?" John asked quizzically.

"Jenny you have studied Baker's tactics, how did that happen?" Vic asked, she anticipated the question.

"I use to freelance in the holiday and business travel industry and I got to know about some of Baker's dirty tricks from people who know him and regretted having dealings with him through his 'Sunrise' travel business. On one occasion I met him at a cocktail party. I must stop now because that will lead me into a long story. I'll tell you later" she said politely smiling. Vic's eyes stares at Jenny, the promise 'later'. He saw an opportunity to invite her to dinner. Mr Hardwick interjects.

"We also have our intelligence systems, we pick up snippets of information from many places and many sources like odd pieces of jigsaw puzzles, if we can fit them together we have a picture. If we have only half of a picture with a little intelligence reckoning we can figure the rest. We read the local newspapers in particular: ex soldiers seeking employment". Vic's not pleased.

"I've had enough jibes, now I'm saying something. Over the last 48 hours I've been through a lot and I'm not handing over the car full of drugs without better consideration or payment!" thinking that the authorities could find some way in compensating him for his cooperation, and surrendering a car full of drugs.

"Yes of course you've been beaten up by rivals attempting to grab the car," said Hardwick without the least bit of sympathy in his voice. He'd had a flash of inspiration.

"We don't pass over the car to Baker; we make him compete for the stuff." Surely he will come out for what he believes is his already. If Vic tells him that he has received a substantially better offer Baker must consider it, as he desperately wants the drugs. The streets are crying out for it".

"How?" said Vic "I don't have his phone number or an address".

"No problem, you present the car at the agreed rendezvous and wait events, don't get out of the car until you get a deal in the offering and only with Baker no one else. Tell him you want a quarter of a million pounds cash to complete the deal or you will negotiate with Ken Flowers".

"Me a sitting duck target waiting for a man whom I've never seen"

"Jenny can describe him, she's seen the man and you spoke to him yesterday evening, you wouldn't forget his voice so soon, would you?"

The Lesser Evil

THE RISK

"So I'm to be the lure to trap this man Baker. We demand a high reward for the contraband before handing over the car, isn't that it?"

Vic smiled contemptuously looking directly at John Hardwick.

"Yes that's basically the plan, we must get the car into Baker's hand before we can take action against him."

"We, you mean me don't you?" Jenny's eyes met his, he saw concern and fear in hers.

"I'll be along to give what assistance you might need" she said

"No thanks... I'll do this one alone, I don't want the responsibility of looking out for anybody other than myself. Remember previously you said Baker was a dangerous man." Those words echoed in his head. He realised that she was concerned for his safety. He saw her as a trim and proper civil servant. Now he has feelings for her as a woman and she sees that in his eyes and feels it in his tone of voice. Vic studied Hardwick face and said,

"Whilst we have been discussing this matter my mind has been working on a plan that could work out with a little co-operation all round. It might be risky, even dangerous, but in my time I've faced many dangers, wartime soldiering is no picnic. Here's what I have in mind."

"If the car is driven to the previously agreed venue at Southampton somebody will appear eventually to take over albeit a day late, it will be reasonable to assume that the person will not be Baker."

The Lesser Evil

Turning his attention away from John Hardwick, he looked at Jenny.

"Jenny you know our target. I will require you to tell me everything you can about Baker and his associates but not just now, later". Turning again to John Hardwick.

"Can you arrange for the car to be bugged, a tracking signal device to be followed by a Helicopter?" John nodded recognition.

"I intend to deliver this car but only into the hand of Baker himself. He will attend an open field of a private estate where I shall have adequate vision all around to allow me to see and deal with any tricks or sudden attacks. He will only know me by meeting me at the time and place designated not more than one hour before hand. He will be required to be seen arriving alone in an open type car, such as an open Land Rover in which there will be a quarter of a million pounds in bank notes to be exchanged for the estate car and the cocaine. I will be able to observe the vehicle approaching from my standpoint about 600 yards away across an open field. He will know that if he pulls a gun on me or attempts any violent action I will have in my hand a device that will detonate explosive charges placed within the car from more than 50 yards distance." Vic looked up to see bewilderment on their faces they were having trouble taking it in, before anybody spoke he continued.

"Of course there will be no explosives only a fake box with words, High Explosives, only I will know that. When the exchange takes place I will quickly check the cash whilst standing a distance away from the car and Baker, I'll take the sham box and place it in the vehicle he came in. tell him to drive the estate car a distance to check it over and leave the other vehicle here in the field to be collected later. The deal being done. Baker can leave with his prize. Being aware that Baker's vehicle maybe booby-trapped, I will not touch it, and I shall remain stranded until the helicopter comes in to pick me up and we follow the estate car signal."

Jenny had butterflies in her belly she could see that there could be no part in his plan for her, she was afraid for him,

"It's very risky, daring, it could succeed." She looked worried- turning to John Hardwick "What do you think?"

"I'll go for it; such a crazy scheme it could work with Vic's military experience and field tactics. I can see why you want the car monitored;

it can be followed to its final destination. There is a serious weakness in your scheme; mostly you will be out of touch and on your own, if anything goes wrong we cannot come charging in like cavalry to help, you must understand that."

"Thanks, I understand the situation. I'll do this job alone and where possible keep you informed of every intended move and the exact location with a map reference."

The trio discussed, modified ideas and made plans building respect and trust between themselves, not aware that it's late afternoon. John Hardwick seemed at least content with the progress made and said,

"I'll give you a tracking signal device tomorrow morning. It's a small simple magnetic clamping box of technology emitting impulse signals with a range of about 30 miles, the battery duration about 18 hours. It could be safely placed under the car bonnet and you'd better carry one in your pocket so that we will know where you are."

"That's what I'd like." He turned to Jenny, smiling she nods in agreement "you said you would tell me all that is known about Baker. I would like to listen to everything, if you will be my guest at dinner tonight?" Astonished she looked towards John Hardwick, he nodded in approval before she answered.

"It's up to you if you wish to have a working dinner, you will be a team on this assignment, go ahead enjoy it. Now I must get back to the office, Jenny, contact me tomorrow." He said, leaving them at the table.

Seeing the question upon her lips "you may choose the rendezvous, time and place to pick you up." Vic said in expectation.

"Wait a minute I've not yet agreed to go anywhere with you for dinner, I have so much to arrange and get ready, it would be an awful rush". But the idea appealed to her.

"Would it be better to simply book our dinner here?"

"No, I'll have to go home to change and liven up a bit, you wouldn't want a dull team mate would you?" She had indirectly agreed to dine with him.

"May I ask where I shall tell the taxi to pick you up?" Her face lights up.

The Lesser Evil

"You've tricked me into this", she smiled, her eyes shining, "lets say 7.30 at Hartley Town Mansion, flat 14 on the Poole sandbanks road, its about 2 miles away".

It was raining heavily when the taxi arrived at Jenny's residence, within a moment she appeared wearing a hooded raincoat and dashed into the cab her perfume preceding her, she said "To the Commodore restaurant". The cabby knew exactly where to go.

"You'll love this place, its nice, quiet atmosphere and good food" she said as they entered the foyer, she moves quickly to the ladies room. "This way Mr. Brandon," the waiter said leading on ahead. He was pleased to see a nicely set out table for two and noticed the place had a dance floor, a stage for musicians and very soft lighting. He had not yet sat when she arrived. He heaved a breath; a surge of excitement lifted his ego. He looked closer, her hair soft flowing, whereas before it was up and tucked in at the back now shining auburn gold. Her eyes bright and beautiful exuding well-being, a flawless complexion and sincere expression upon her lips with a slight tinge of a smile. Could this be the woman, the staid civil servant he'd met earlier that day; was she the one he briefly encountered in the German court?

"Are you not going to offer a lady a drink?" she asked to snap him out of his astonishment.

"Yes, of course yes. Sorry I was overcome by the dramatic change, you look so different. May I suggest a bottle of wine with our dinner?

"Yes but for now I would like a Martini with Ice." she said to the waiter, standing close by.

"You sir, what would you like?"

"I'll have a Brandy and dry ginger, no ice"

"The wine for your dinner sir?" His eyes still upon Jenny, only half hearing the waiter "The wine sir?" She replies

"Ladies choice, White wine French Beaujourlais." Wow! She even speaks differently, he loved the way she spoke those words in French. 'I suppose you speak the language well?' she smiled at the compliment.

"I wasn't long was I? I mean getting ready."

"Not at all, right on time." The drinks arrived; he raised his glass to her and saw her hazel eyes shining. The same eyes that disturbed him

42

when he met them for the first time in court in Dusseldorf. It was as if she were two persons. He preferred the one sitting with him at their table. They had ordered from the menu, eating hungrily, enjoying their food and each other's company, raising his eye again to her, he mentioned

"The waiter knew my name, did you phone in to book our table?"

"Yes I realised you might not know the best places to eat so I booked this place in your name."

"You're wonderful, I would not have thought of that, not being in the habit of taking ladies out to dinner, Thank you." He saw in her polite smile, she wanted the evening to be a comfortable, successful occasion. He gently touched her hand, he could have kissed her.

"I have a lot to tell you and there's much you should know. This is a working dinner, remember". She realised he was flirting with her and in her mind she encouraged it.

"Jenny, you are a mystery to me, some how you don't fit into your role as a customs officer, yet you act the part well and then turn up here to astonish me, a completely different person". She cast an intelligent glance towards him.

"I'll explain everything when the table is cleared". He emptied the wine bottle into their glasses; the waiter cleared everything away. Vic eagerly awaits her story.

The Lesser Evil

JUGGERNAUT   VIC

JUGGERNAUT

"Five years ago at the accomplished age of twenty two I landed a job with a travel agency and within a year promoted to courier travelling aboard various cruise ships and sometimes ferryboats. Upon my third cruise I met Tony Robbin a man 5 years my senior, handsome, gentle personality an own account businessman freighting merchandise from eastern Europe into and out of England with an articulated vehicle and trailer, juggernauts they called them; His lorry could carry 20 tons pay load. Each trip was very profitable, 2 times weekly was possible. I fell in love with him and we married 6 months later but I didn't give up my job. Cruising in the Mediterranean as courier with a famous shipping line assisting parties of businessmen and women. I was sometimes invited to an onboard private party. Upon one such occasion the host, a flamboyant over indulgent man, past middle age with smooth personality invited me to join him. His name 'Reggie Baker' I didn't take to him although he chatted me up making me feel welcome. He asked about my work and gave me his business card 'Sunrise Travel Agents, Call me when you're next in Bournemouth to talk about your career'. He entertained me twice again but I avoided further meetings because of his overbearing affection for me. When I told my husband about Reggie Baker and described him, Tony said he was often carrying merchandise for Baker international haulage. 'Falkon Freights is another Baker company. Months later Tony was in Torino Italy to haul into England 3000 cases of wine. He backed

44

his lorry into a factory yard for overnight loading ready for early morning start. He was accommodated in a local hotel less than a mile away." She said; and spoke seriously as if giving evidence in court, something on her mind hurt her . She stopped, sighed and continued;

"After dinner Tony, taking the night fresh air walked down to the lorry loading yard to get documents from the vehicle cab. A forklift truck carrying palletised cases of wine for loading drove along the vehicle side and turned sharply at the rear causing two cases to topple to the ground, one case broke open, smashing a bottle. Hurriedly three men scuffled to clear up the damage and swept away everything else. Tony's offer to help was abruptly refused. 'Unusual suspicious behaviour' he thought, so he grabs a bottle only to have it snatched from his hand by a big man waving his arms indicating he should leave now and he turned to leave. The men spoke in their own language aggressively and with anger at each other about the occurrence. Tony was determined to find out what was happening. In the dim light, unseen he slipped in under the back axle of the trailer urged himself towards the forklift truck. Whilst the men were still talking he sneaked a bottle from the broken case and made a quick exit towards the street and the hotel. In the bedroom he opened the bottle. It was not wine; it smelt funny, pungent and tasted sour to the tongue. He's sure the men were loading these bottles on to his truck, contraband of which he should not be aware. He had heard stories of illegal drugs and substances being stowed away aboard heavy goods vehicles without drivers knowing. The customs official carrying out spot checks finding illegal imports, the culprits suffering severe penalties, a long term prison sentence was not unusual.

Thoughts raised in his mind. His contract, to carry 3000 cases of wine from Italy to a distribution point in north Dorset at an agreed price for R.A Baker. He had heard it said in conversation that Baker had been accused of smuggling a long time ago. He shuddered at the thought that in the past year he had hauled many loads into England for the same man perhaps with some contraband secretly stowed aboard. This load he will declare to the customs upon arrival in Dover. Realising that the customs will examine documents and each wine case in the consignment on board the lorry, he will be required to give a full account statement. He knows

45

they can impound his vehicle also. These things will mean long delays and late getting home, he must inform Jenny. He phoned from the bedside, the hotel reception and got a U.K call through to Bournemouth. I was asleep when the phone rang, looking at the bedside clock it was near eleven I was surprised to hear Tony's voice. He spoke in a matter-of-fact way and related everything I have told you." Her eyes drooped sadly, tears glistened. Putting her face in her hands she sighed and took a long breath, she was reliving the trauma of nearly two years ago, finding it difficult to speak between heaving breaths she was trying to say something like:- "That's the, the last words…he spoke to me…he's dead."! She remained, head in her hands, Vic gave her his handkerchief… "I'll get you another Martini"…. He handed it to her, trying to cheer her up. She lifted her eyes to his. "You understand my sorrow, if I embarrassed you". "Of course I'm only human". She drinks her martini down, it brings her to life. "Please get me another?" she asked: she continued with her story.

"Oh yes the phone, he was cut off leaving me believing that he might be home in about 2 days, he would phone again from Dover", I felt some anxiety about the phone call it left me with butterflies in my belly. He never called me late before in such a cold unaffectionate manner, he never phoned from Dover either. On the Monday afternoon a women police constable arrived at the door, I knew something serious had happened. The constable came in and sat down and ask routine identity questions and said "Mrs Robin, your husband we believe was in a fatal road accident on Thursday late evening", I'm perplexed, confused not understanding I just stare at the constable. "We understand the lorry he was driving ran off the road and rolled over. We expect further and better information from the Italian police soon". I somehow expected tragic news, but it didn't make it any easier to bear.

"Are you living alone? Would you like someone to talk with you?" Gradually the word fatal enters my mind with all its consequences, "You mean he's dead, Tony's dead." My mouth quivered hesitantly I was unable to speak "No leave me!"

"We will ask you later to give a statement". The constable was sympathetic and left. I sat numbed, staring at the living room wall remembering Tony and our romantic days together, every time he'd return from a long haul journey we'd be together for a few wondrous days. He always bought me beautiful French underwear and expensive things. Each summer the lorry would be taken off the road for two weeks to be serviced, repaired, tested and checked with techograph, vehicle performance record system. During these two weeks we fled to New York and married by special license, I dreaded his leaving me so often to haul goods across Europe, but that was the business he'd committed so much to, and it began to be profitable, capital was building in our bank account.

The women police constable returned the next day with more sad news. The police found his passport and other such documents, which proved the identity of the body. "There will be an inquest into the accident in the next few days; you might be required to attend". The constable seemed to understand but still asked me to make a statement. The constable wrote down each word I said: "Tony left early on Thursday morning expecting to be aboard the Dover ferry for Calais about 0630 hours. The lorry was empty intending to bring into England wine from Italy the next day. I heard from him next around 11 that night when he phoned from his hotel to tell me that he suspected that some of the bottles which had been loaded during that evening were not wine and that he will declare the load to the customs at Dover which will mean considerable delays returning home". I continued to give details to the constable, who I must ask questions and I nodded approval.

"Mr. Tony Robin phoned you at about eleven saying that his vehicle was loaded with suspect wine bottles and that he intended to declare the load at Dover, do you know the name of the hotel from which he telephoned you and what company loaded the merchandise?"

"The name of the hotel was never mentioned neither was any company named" I replied. The constable continued, she wanted to know because the lorry ran off the road about 2330 hours European time was carrying no load and had apparently not arrived at its intended destination. The accident had occurred about 4 kilometres before the town of Torino on the north side at a place known locally as Condove. The road at that point bends sharply to the left and there the truck crashed through a roadside marker fence, ran a short distance and capsized into a deep ravine rolling over sideways twice before coming to a rest. Initial report shows the

47

driver may have died trying to escape the vehicle as it rolled over upon him. His injuries were consistent with such an accident."

I looked at the policewomen in astonishment: "You mean he never arrived in Torino, had no load upon his lorry and therefore could not have phoned me from his hotel at about eleven because he was already dead." The constable wrote it all into the statement. I was so disturbed I was choking, I could have screamed, but it stuck in my throat, it's ridiculous nonsense, it's all lies, I could think of nothing more to say to the policewomen. I just shook my head not able to answer finding the ordeal too distressing. I wondered what the constable thought as she left? "I'm not lying, its not some fantasy but I can't prove any of it... yet, but I will, I must"

I contacted the customs at Dover told somebody what I knew about the accident and that there may have been some smuggling involved, it was agreed that an official would contact me later that day. I spent the next hour over a coffee, pondering, trying to make sense of the events of the last few days.

Poole Harbour customs office phoned around 2 hours later, I spoke to Mister John Hardwick, he was interested and listened to my story. He wished to interview me and perhaps develop a case file. I was willing to cooperate with the customs, and subsequently gave detailed information with a statement. I learnt that a case study had been opened upon Mister R.A Baker, hearing that name again I felt sure that he was behind Tony's fatal accident. I was pleased to meet Mister Hardwick in his office at Poole, I'd found somebody to listen, understand and perhaps sympathize with me." Vic takes her hand into his, holding it firmly to let her know that he also understands and sympathizes with her. She must continue.

"Mister Hardwick told me that for many months he had been collecting information about Mister Baker's business and other sordid activities. He had frequently run into difficulties with getting reliable witnesses to testify against Mr. Baker and anybody connected with his many dubious affairs. The police must also have files on Baker and his partner in crime Mr Brian Booth, both of them lie to cover each other and have been known to threaten women and intimidate people. One male witness was found dead floating in the harbour 2 days before an important criminal case hearing against one of Bakers associates. Another occasion acid disfigured a girls face to prevent her father from giving evidence. John Hardwick spoke of many other things such as bringing into England girls from Serbia and other parts of Eastern Europe, they were expecting to be au pair girls, they ended up being used in the sex trade as call girls,

('R.Z Baker international haulage contractor seeks own account heavy goods vehicle drivers and operators. Must have clean licence etc'.) This advertisement was placed in a 'Commercial Motor Magazine'; respondents are subsequently invited to a business house party seminar with three or four other interested enterprising lorry drivers, operators. Saturday evening is the usual time and an over night stay is offered at the venue: Veracity Farm House North Dorset. The annexe has 4 separate bedrooms for guests, wives are not catered for. When the men are settled in they meet their hostess Mrs Valerie Baker and discuss their culinary requirements. There's a wide choice of drinks with detailed business propositions and long discussions before settling down to a lavish dinner. Each course is prepared by their hostess who has carefully laced each meal with cocaine effectively making everybody feel comfortable, the guests become indulgent, intoxicated and at this stage the sexy girls are introduced, pairings soon take place and everybody gets excited.

I assured myself that my Tony never attended a house party but he had delivered loaded sealed containers to Veracity Farm. Trailer born containers and articulated trailers were preferred by the Baker operation. A particular container marked for future recognition is about 7 feet inside width and about 15feet length. The double decked floor is fitted with secret under space of about 3 inches. The second floor being precisely made and easily removed provided 26 cubic feet of space for contraband. Containers are transported all over Europe closed and sealed by customs officials under an international agreement T.I.R (Transport International Routies) carriage. Exploiting this system valuable consignments of drugs came into Bakers hands making him very rich and dangerously unscrupulous. The customs eventually discovered the false floors, stopped and opened some containers. That closed the route for bringing in drugs by that method. Two container freighting owner drivers are serving time. Once embarked upon supplying the street trade with drugs one is committed to continue there-on-after and bound to seek ever more means of smuggling the stuff into the country". She said shrugging her shoulders sympathetically towards Vic. " That's where you come into the story Vic, before I continue I'm sure you realise that Baker is a dangerous man, he will not fall for any tricks. I fear for you with your intended negotiations, he is evil". Vic could see she was genuinely concerned for his safety.

"You were going to give me a full description of this man I shall meet?"

"All together I've met him about three times, I've also had time and opportunity to study the custom's dossier held upon him. His true name is Reginald Lesser. He trades under the name Baker, perhaps because it gives a better image. He has also used the name James Joyce; he's about 45, dresses in the style of a younger man, stands about 5ft 10ins, clean shaven with neatly groomed, semi long dark hair, slightly overweight, fresh complexion with brown eyes. He loves company and talking. Two distinguishing features: he's short sighted, too vain to wear his special glasses, and he gets close to people in conversation, this would have exempted him military service also he smokes expensive cigars". Vic listened to all her words as a student attends the master; he builds a mental image of the man she describes. It enters his mind that perhaps she is seeking vengeance and retribution for her tragic loss, and why not?. The accident that made her a widow greatly disturbed her life, she could feel it in her soul that Baker was in someway behind it.

"Upon our initial meeting, John Hardwick asked me many questions about Tony's haulage business. He also inquired into my career background, which seemed to interest him. He studied my face carefully asking: Would you like to help investigate your husband's demise by attending the accident enquiry in Torino with myself? Among other things you may be required to identify the body". The thought of seeing my lover dead caused my whole body to quake, I believed I could not do it…

"We can offer you employment as a clerical assistant you will also be able claim expenses of course". "I jumped at that opportunity. It took many months before I became John Hardwick's personal assistant and that is my position now, I'm not a customs officer." she said.

50

V J Tarry

John Hardwick made plans for me to attend the hearing with himself in Torino some 21 days later. The court was held in an annexe to the local police headquarters. Presiding was a magistrate with a court recorder, in attendance an official from the department of roads and highways and a medical examiner. Also there was a reporter from the local news and 8 or 9 other members of the public. I frequently cast my eye around the court taking careful notes of everything and everybody but recognised no individual person. The proceeding were opened and continued in the Italian language much to my disadvantage. Identity of the deceased was established by a passport and other documents. The police report established the time of the accident 2330 hours. The driver was Anthony James Robin. The road surface good, weather fine, clear night, no skid marks. The lorry was in good condition at the time of the incident no defect to explain the cause of accident; it rolled over twice, serious damage resulted. It was presumed that having travelled a long way from England the driver fell asleep and ran off the road. John was also taking notes he understood some of the language: most distressing was the evidence from the medical examiner explaining how the very serious head injuries were the primary cause of death. No question was asked about bruising not consistent with the accident, was his blood tested for drugs or alcohol? I understood enough to cause me to shudder in despair. No witness came forward to offer any other evidence. The road was not much used at night, there was no roadside lighting. The proceedings lasted about an hour and closed with a verdict of accidental death. The only newspaper reporter was watching myself and John throughout the proceedings. Before I could rise from my seat the man approached us both "Pardon Madame, sir, I am Mark Stephenelli from the 'Torino' news". He offers his business card "the lady is a distressed widow from this accident: yes? I wish to help you as much as I can" he said, John was pleased that somebody spoke English and in particular a newspaper reporter who would help. Looking at his card he rose to ask him if he made notes of everything in the court. Yes he did make a report. He wished to discuss the accident background with me; he thinks I can give him another story, better and more interesting than the routine court proceeding report and that he can help me very much. He had an intelligent nose for a good story. "You use my name Mark: please" he requested. John who had appeared incognito said he wished to see all the documentary evidence in this case accident. He asked Mark to advise and direct his interest. "You come, we go talk to the recorder he will have everything".

"Mark takes me by my hand quickly to the man clearing away papers and things. All documents were displayed but more important I found no consignment notes for carriage of goods, no route card, he always makes a route card, no Taco-graph records of the lorries journey times and distance covered. I expected to find fuel bills, hotel bills and restaurant account slips. He was meticulous about keeping his accounts and records correctly in a locked metal box in the vehicle cab, that box was not mentioned, not found." she said.

"Mark listened to my story over a cup of coffee he made short hand notes of everything that was said, my story intrigued him. To find the hotel from which my husband phoned on that fatal night would be near impossible. There were 26 small hotels listed in the local telephone book, would any hotel show their telephone accounts recording a call to England on that said date?" John interjected, "The British telephone system does not record calls to private residents from abroad, the only hope is at this end. We must find the particular hotel, without it we cannot prove anything". Suddenly John asked "Who recovered the vehicle from the crash site and where is it? We wish to inspect it" Mark, without answers looked blank. "I remembered I told his insurance company the day after the police constable told me of the fatal accident. I gave them all the details required and was advised that the police would give them further information. The insurance company will arrange for the vehicle to be recovered back to England... that was over four weeks ago. I heard nothing from the insurance company since."

Mark suggested we go to the police to find the lorry. Explaining to a policeman that the lady was the driver's widow and she wished to see the lorry in which her man died. After establishing identity they gave me a paper with the name and address of the garage believed to have recovered the lorry, the accident site was also given by map reference and name 'condove'. Mark drove us to the garage and soon we were looking over the grossly distorted, damaged vehicle and its trailer. The recovery operation took two days to get the salvage up out of the 60 metre deep ravine. The police looked over every part of the lorry and trailer and an insurance examiner had gone through it also. He had said the vehicle and its trailer were beyond economical repair. Staring at the smashed up damaged cab I remembered that our time together after he returned from a long haul would be wonderful. I got an urge to sit in the driver's seat. The cab door had been wrenched off; the step was bent up but that didn't stop me. I hadn't climbed into his lorry before and now I felt closer and alone with him there silently reminiscing feeling… Looking around inside everything had been stripped out of the cab: the bunk bed behind the driver seat was gone, all his various tools and equipment were missing. The vehicle had been systematically ransacked everything taken. Scavengers cleared everything of value. I settled upon the drivers seat, marvelled that it was still in place. The windscreen although shattered from corner to corner was in place secure. Lifting my head up a little I moved the drivers sun visor down without a thought my eyes seized upon a strip of paper tucked in the flap. Behind it I found several business cards and a letter 'Hotel Vigliana' alerted my mind, other cards were routine business. The letter written in long hand dated the same day as the accident, more in the form of a route giving directions from Calais to Torino with advice about best times to travel etc mentioned hotel Vigliana, I examined the business card, the address three words stood out bold "Torino. Hotel Vigliana"; I felt sure this is what I was looking for. In my head I could hear Tony talking to me on the telephone from that hotel, the last words he said to me, "I love you, goodnight darling". John and Mark were taking photographs of the damaged lorry unit and its trailer a few paces away. Excited, I called the men to attend me. There was urgency in my voice and both sped to my side. "Look what I found under the visor" passing the card to John with Mark looking to see it also. "I feel it in my heart and soul that is the hotel".

Mark thought he knew the whereabouts of the hotel Vigliana, about 8 kilometres away, and would take us. John hesitated "If we go into the hotel asking questions somebody might get suspicious. People have gone to a lot of trouble to cover all traces of the accident and it would be better to leave things like that for the moment. The people concerned will feel better secure knowing the court verdict now. However firstly we should try to find the accident site. "Mark do you know where the accident happened?" John asked. Mark was able to learn from the recovery operator where the crash site was.

"I'll look it up on my road map; it cannot be far away".

"Please find the place, I must go there, please take me". I pleaded. My heart was reaching out to the place. Tony would want me to see it. We drove through some picturesque hilly landscape scenery to come to a site cordoned off by police markers.

"This must be it" Mark said as he parked just off the road a little further along in a safe place. I was first out of the car and ran back to a point where it was easiest to look down into the ravine where Tony and his lorry came to an end. Staring down into the hollow, winds whistled and whispered to me up from the depth, it sent shivers of horror through me. Haunted by the scene I stood frozen to the spot, my mind wildly imagining everything that had happened on that fatal night. I could feel it in every fibre in my body, Tony my first love did not die in that hollow, he was murdered. I turned to see Mark and John standing silently either side of me looking into a deep ravine, sharing my grief.

"He was murdered, I know it. I think I knew it all along". John puts his arm around my shoulder giving support and comfort. He then took many photographs of the site and quietly said.

"We cannot do anything more here, come let's move on".

Reverently we moved to enter the car, it slowly drove away; as if in a funeral cortège.

I asked Mark to take us just to see the hotel from the outside. Minutes later we were motoring along a secondary road parallel to a motorway about 200 metres to our right in a rural area the road turned to underpass the motorway moving north. A little more then 1 kilometre along this road we drove slowly into the forecourt of the hotel Vigliana. A small hotel of about 15 bedrooms and a large parking area with a gravel surface suitable for heavy vehicles. John noticed its position placed it ideally for drivers overnight stays; he takes photographs without leaving the car. Suddenly John takes off his coat and tie rolls up his shirt sleeves, dishevelled his hair and swaggers into the entrance, returning 5 minutes later with a hotel tariff and business card. Pointing out the card he got showed the printers code date the same as the one from the lorry proving they are both of recent issues. The manager spoke to him in English with a Scottish accent which was surprising because he looked every bit like an Italian. Mark begins to see an intriguing story developing and busied himself, making detailed notes, asking me about the phone message.

"Did you say the loading yard was about 1 mile away from the hotel?"

"Tony told me on the fatal night he had walked about 1 mile down to the yard, where they were loading his lorry".

"This road goes down, lets have a look," Mark said.

As we drove slowly down towards the motorway underpass the road-side was covered in hedged shrubbery. A wide gap appeared through which an entrance road takes our eyes to a small complex of industrial buildings. Mark drove into the place slowly whilst we observed each building through to the end stop. He was turning the car to exit when I said aloud. "That's it, there above over the factory entrance" I pointed to a big industrial sign displayed to be seen from the motorway about 60 metres away "International Freight Forwarding Organisation", that must be it and there's the yard alongside where Tony reversed his vehicle for loading". John photographed the building and the sign separately as the car moved away to stop in the car parking area. He thought it better not to be seen lingering near that factory. I was full of enthusiasm and said "I knew we would find the place I just knew it". John, dampening down my enthusiasm said "Now lets consider what we have ".

1, a letter (unsigned) directing a person (unnamed) from Calais to Torino dated the same day as the fatal accident. That letter must have been put into Tony's hand before he left England, question; by whom?

2, a hotel business card referring to hotel Vigliana is found in his vehicle cab. Question; did Tony put the card in the flap behind the sun visor after he walked back to the lorry from the hotel, or did somebody give it to him before leaving Dover or another time?

3, the factory displaying the bold sign in English words seem to be the place where his lorry was being loaded with suspect wine bottles.

The Lesser Evil

4, Jenny said Tony spoke to her from a hotel about one mile from the loading place. Hotel Vigliana and the factory are about one mile apart.

5, Jenny also said the phone call she received came in about eleven (2300 hours) English time that would be midnight in Italy.

6, the police recorded the accident time at circa 2330 hours, local time, no witness came forward to confirm any time.

7, No tacho-graph records were found within the wreckage. New European law required all heavy goods vehicle drivers to make proper journey records over every 24 hours by changing the recording disc inside the instrument daily.

There are two vital parts missing: The telephone call record

The tachograph records.

If either came to light we could go to the police and get the case re-examined".

Mark wrote down everything in the order John said it.

"The hotel telephone number is on the card, can I see it"? He asked.

I saw a spark of inspiration in his eye; eagerly I pass the card to him and await a response. He copies the hotel telephone number into his notebook; Mark can see the story he's after developing.

"I would like to try something; my girlfriend is employed with Murcery International Telecommunications: she's a wizard with these new computers. I would ask her, "nicely of course", to help locate any calls from the hotel's number to England on or about 2330 hours on the night in question, perhaps she can do that?"

"Her duty starts 2 to 10 this month, she should be in her office about now. I'll take you to your hotel and from their telephone to get any information about calls from the hotel Vigliana.

Mark left us in our hotel to attend to other business whilst afternoon coffee was served. I seemed to glow with enthusiasm and drank another cup. My alert mind was digesting everything we learnt, it gave me a new found confidence and zest.

"That hotel is the seat of Tony's death," I told myself. In my mind I could clearly see the set up: Lorries bringing and taking goods across Europe would find it economically convenient to stay overnight taking up bed and breakfast at the nearest recommended hotel. Loads for tran-
56

sit to England would be given special interest by 'International Freight Organisation' offering trans shipment services, or just overnight staging. They would check the tyre pressures, fill up the fuel tanks and generally get the lorry ready for an early morning start. The driver would be well looked after at the hotel one mile up the road. In the course of routine chatting over dinner matters to do with loads, journeys and destinations would be unwittingly given in light conversation and carefully noted. During the quiet hours illegal drugs could be stowed away in places within the cargo carrying vehicle or it's trailer unknown to the driver. Consignment note with destination would be given with other routine documents. I was able to direct my thoughts to see the infinite possibilities of smuggling contraband around Europe and into the United Kingdom by using the numerous juggernauts towing trailers. It would have to be well organised from a central source using many depots. It would take a mastermind, a man with a flare for business, cunning and treachery. I could think of only one man with all the necessary attributes, a man with evil in his soul; 'Lesser' known to be trading as Baker International Transport she added for her own satisfaction the words: criminal organisation.

I turned to see John sitting opposite me looking bewildered, staring into the distance he was harmonizing his thoughts.

"Penny for your thoughts?" I said

"Oh! I'm sorry I was miles away thinking about all the lorries moving about and crossing frontiers carrying everything for industries and everything we buy in our high street shops. It's only a small percentage of the many thousand of lorries crossing borders that are checked for contraband. To do the job thoroughly unloading the vehicle, perhaps opening package cases and examining the vehicle structure. The delay would mean certain foods decaying it could never be practical. The smugglers know that and often take risks because they reckon the chances of not being caught are much in their favour.

"Your husband was an honest man. When he discovered the load upon his lorry was not wine, and perhaps a narcotic substance intended for the English drug trade, he threatened to surrender the whole consignment to the customs at Dover. That threat would have brought him into direct conflict with the smugglers therefore he was murdered to prevent any further inquiries taking place. This is the sort of thing done by the Mafia. Many people have had accidents or are found dead without adequate reason or explanation. The Mafia in this part of Italy is involved with nearly everything criminal. It would not have been difficult for their organisation to arrange an accident at short notice. The legal profession in Italy is frequently impeded in their work because of the insidious secret activities of the Mafia and this can influence and restrict the court proceedings in many ways. The criminal justice system does not work well here that's why I prefer to remain incognito".

I listening to every word John said, I now felt less enthusiastic about getting some form of retribution for my husbands' murder.

Wondering what to do next I asked, "Could we get the case opened in England?"

"I think not. There is insufficient conclusive evidence and it would not be practical to summon anybody to attend a criminal court in England even if you could find a competent solicitor willing to take up a case of this nature on your behalf". John said.

I heaved a breath of forlorn hope and sighed, I'm deflated. For the time being I wished to drop the matter. I stood up and said.

"We must leave the hotel early tomorrow morning, I'll start packing now, and shall I see you at dinner later?"

We were nearly through our first course meal when a waiter attended the table with an envelope for Madame Robin.

It was from Mark: a simple note with no information but two telephone numbers with the date and time of calls from the hotel Vigliana at 0056 hours the other at 0148 hours. This was great news.

I stood up smartly; I wanted to shout enhancing my belief I knew they would find that I received the telephone call from Tony just before he was killed. Pointing to the note I passed it to John.

"That's our phone number, the first one there is the number he called from the hotel to talk to me at home. John was pleased for me but could not in the same way share my joy at finding the origin of my husbands last phone call, it was something tragically mournful for me. He turned his interest towards the other telephone number from the hotel to England.

That number must surely identify somebody. He intends to pursue inquiries immediately they return home, he's eager to know who answers at the end of that telephone line.

"Now we know."

"Tony was not dead at 2330 as the police report alleged because he spoke to me at 2356 hours English time. It now seems most likely that some person in the hotel listened to the call Tony made to me about surrendering the load to the customs at Dover. He would have been confronted and not yielding was beaten to death, the accident arranged to cover up everything, but how could the police get the timing wrong?"

"You will remember that the accident was not discovered until the following morning. There was no witness and the scene could have been adjusted to give the impression that the accident happened earlier, also the body would be cold by the following morning". John said. The thought made me shiver.

"Another thing, according to reports there was no freight container, no load upon the trailer, how long would it take to unload 3000 cases of wine and move the trailer to the accident site and then wreck it? There's one possibility comes to mind: it was not his trailer. These juggernaut vehicles with their trailer towing systems that include braking, lighting are often interconnect-able with the modern road transport vehicle. It therefore becomes possible for any towing vehicle to tow many different trailers as long as they connect up correctly! Before I could ask a question, John continued looking to me "Do you know the make, type and chassis number of Tony's trailer?"

"No! I never saw it. When he was towing other trailers his was kept in some goods vehicle park somewhere near Dover. We can get the necessary information from his insurance company when we return home".

John looked at me, his mind pondering the question. He said: "if what I suspect is true then Tony's loaded trailer is in the hands of smugglers and murderers. We must return to the garage where the wreckage is kept to get details of that particular trailer and its chassis number".

The next morning we were both packed to leave early. Our flight to England had been delayed, now scheduled to leave at 1430 hours. Mark walked into the hotel as John was clearing our account.

59

The Lesser Evil

"Am I pleased to see you", John said, "I would like to thank you and your lady friend for sending details of the telephone calls from the hotel Vigliana". He smiled and winked.

"You must be mistaken I sent nothing". Understanding his wish not to be involved, John replied. "Of course not, we're discreet". Mark passes on an envelope. "I do have something for you, photographs of the accident wreckage". Each was very clear showing details of the trailer damage; one showing the two axles were almost completely wrenched out of the chassis of the trailer in the accident. John looked closely, a photograph showed very clearly along the trailer platform side rail R.B.4. He passes it to me, and points to the two letters R.B. and number 4. I saw what he was thinking "Yes that could only be Reginald Bakers trailer number 4" every time something is discovered I tingle with delight at the find.

"Mark these photographs are very helpful and we are obliged to you for your assistance. We hope you get your story together soon".

"I am reluctant to ask you to assist us further," John said, tongue in cheek, hoping for a favourable response!"

"Mark you took us where the vehicle and trailer wreckage is laying therefore you know where to go and I must return to get more details from the vehicle and trailer". He never finished what he had in mind to say. Mark immediately responds; "OK lets go".

Half an hour later we again enter the garage yard to view the reclaimed wrecks. The trailer was being dismembered, it had been turned upside down and both axles taken out. The trailer plate recording all information including make, type, chassis number had been obviously, and recently chiselled off, no where to be found and no explanation given. Mark with camera alert, was flashing at all interesting angles photographing both dismantled vehicles, John was doing much the same thing. I was trying to speak to one of the workmen, conversation progressed tediously, Mark stepped into help me.

"What are you asking, can I help you?" I pointing to the trailer body side rail where RB4 had been, but only abrasive scrub marks remain! "Ask him who removed the letters and the number."

Mark looks round the other side and saw nothing amiss, returns to speak to one man. I walked to the main towing vehicle to remember it was
60

completely re-serviced, instruments calibrated and professionally tested about six months ago. Now it stands in a muddy yard in a badly damaged and vandalised condition. Hatred was building in my heart. My dreams of a happy future together with Tony, my 'knight of the highways' and myself lay in ruins. I must face it all alone, vengeance was seizing my heart.

Mark stood silently besides me seeing, feeling and understanding my grief. "The workmen are only doing their job they know nothing about the letters or the number." I turned to Mark "You have been very kind to help us so much. We need to go to the police station next to collect a few things and report our departure, will that be on your way?" I asked.

The police constable gave me all that was found of Tony's things including his blood stained clothing, all thrown into an official paper bag.

He must surely have had money but none was recovered. As I received the bag a pain stabbed at my heart, I had to come to Torino to find the facts, now I was willing myself to leave without delay. Mark spoke with the constable and replied to me.

"You must go to the crematorium to collect your husband's ashes," he said. I turned away my face pale in distress. I looked at John and said "Please get me out of here! Please take me home!"....

"Vic you have been very patient with me, indulging myself in my story. You had to know everything; it's for your own ultimate safety. I want you to know how I feel about the evil Bakers and the hatred he left within me". "Know your enemy" he mused.

She drank the last of her fourth Martini, looking around the restaurant most guests had left. She noticed that one man stood at the bar drinking. He turned to raise his glass in a gesture towards her. She knew the man, but chose to ignore him. Vic also noticed the man; his bearing led him to think that he might have been in Her Majesties Service at one time.

"Who's that?" Vic asked.

"He's Simon Sinclair, ex navy commander, and now a customs officer with the Poole Harbour Authority. I never liked him from our first meeting. His handshake felt cold, his eyes devious and there's something about him that I can't explain. I think he's a philanderer".

Vic emptied his glass, whilst asking the waiter to call a taxi for them. She smiled wearily, closed her eyes, trying to collect her thoughts. "It's been a long day for both of us. We are a team" She said as they left. The taxi stops outside the entry door to a block of flats. Vic moved to open the cab door. As she got was getting out of the taxi he lifted her up, she faltered, unsteady and toppled into his arms and then he kissed her. They knew it would happen, they hugged each other, their lingering kiss sealing the partnership between them. He felt anxiety in her body, he saw it in her eyes, she's afraid.

"Both you and I know why you want to come inside with me, but even if I wanted to, I wouldn't let you. So please don't ask".

"Did I do something wrong?"

"I had a great day, an interesting, wonderful day. Actually it's the best day I've had for a long time, you understand?"

"Then what is it?"

"You've been giving me full attention and flirting with me all day. Don't think that I don't like it, we know what'll happen if I let you through the door. No, not now, we both have a full programme for tomorrow. There will be other times".

"You're right" He admitted and forced a smile, "Let's call it a night".

When he took a small step backward, she caught his eye.

"Thank you", she turned, and after an awkward pause, walked to the door. She could feel his disappointment. She turned again, and said "I'll be drinking coffee in Gordon's tomorrow. Good night".....

The Lesser Evil

OPENING SHOT

Vic was awakened early the next morning. Ravens or crows were squawking in the tree tops level with his window, a mating season contest? He throws the bedroom window open wide, fills his lungs, exhales and said to the birds, "She loves me". That made him feel good to start the day. He was nearly through breakfast when John Hardwick phoned to make arrangement to fit the estate car with a monitor bugging device. He also wished to finalise details for the days venture. They talked together for a few minutes. Vic would have preferred Jenny.

It was a bright sunny morning when he set out. He walked to the multi-storey car park where he'd left the estate car. Walking gave him leisure and freedom to go over his plan, and adjust his mind to the forthcoming engagement. He must get none other than Mister Reginald Lesser to take possession of the car load of cocaine in exchange for fifty thousand pounds cash. Of course Lesser will be reluctant to enter into any such transaction. Therefore it will be expected of him that he will employ any of a bag of dirty tricks, not stopping short of murder. Vic finds himself marching with determination to achieve his goal. Each marching step hammers into his mind the will to succeed for himself and to avenge Jenny's tragic loss and hurt. They were two of a kind who could give each other comfort. It's a feeling he couldn't explain, it drove his resolve. He met John and another man at the car park entrance. The estate car had stood secure overnight, was opened up for the workman to fit the monitoring device.

John produced a radio mobile telephone operating on a fixed frequency so that they could keep in contact with each other. The same system used by taxi and lorry drivers to keep in touch. "It's the 'Citizen's Band Radio', you clip that onto your belt, it'll be more secure there, you don't want to loose it!"

John saw that Vic was resolute and ready to face the challenge he had set himself. After checking everything, he looked to John, offering his hand "Goodbye, see you soon"

Driving toward Southampton, listening to the car radio, Vic Brandon was pleased to hear the weather is going to be fine and sunny for the next two days. "Good, that's good" he said aloud to himself. Entering the suburbs of the town he is looking out for, and finds a second-hand junk shop, and purchases a small overnight case, and a hand held light thumb press switch with a long length electric light flexible cable. He's well pleased with what he bought, and continues his journey to Southampton Airport car park.

The estate car is stopped as he attempts to enter the parking lot. Mister Sladen steps to the car side and said

"You're over a day late, everybody is getting anxious, wondering what kept you so long. The car park's full, you will be able to move your own car, and put this one in it's' place". Sladen was already moving to give direction as he spoke. He must have been told what to do previously, and he knew that this particular car was important. Vic just sits, without moving a wheel. Sladen returns to open the car door to make himself better heard and understood.

"If you follow my direction, I take you!" He never finished.

Vic interjected a definite "NO, I'm not putting the car in here!"

"But you must, that's my instruction. You must put the estate car in place of your own car, and leave."

"No, you get on the phone and tell your boss that I am not putting the estate car into his reach until I am satisfied that better terms and payments are agreed upon, and that now I'll sit here waiting." He felt like a sergeant again giving orders. The car-park attendant could see that every word was a command, he moved urgently to his box office to speak upon a telephone, returning in some haste to say, "Mister Baker wants to talk to you straight away."

"No, I'm not leaving this car to talk to anyone, pass the phone to me now!"

"I don't think the line will reach to your car, even if you moved it closer"

"Then tell him I'll phone him later, get the telephone number"

Sladen, annoyed, returns to say "Mister Baker is already in a temper over your delay, he will soon send somebody along to talk to you, in about half an hour."

Vic sat waiting thinking about Jenny, her genuine concern for his safety. He recalls her emotions and sadness as she related her story the previous night at dinner, yet she still had heart and feeling for him. Ever since his school boy days he's had nobody personally concerned about his well being. He remembers returning home on a late winter's day to be told that both Mum and Dad were lost at sea. They were returning from South America aboard the steamer 'Baldair'. It was reported lost at sea in the early days of the war. He spent the next two years in 'The Wandsworth trust' residential school in north London. At the age 16 ½ he's enlisted into 'The Coldstream Guards' and subsequently became an efficient infantry man, fighting where needed in war zones. "Yes, young man, this is the life for you, there's a career ahead for a man of your calibre" they said. What ever that meant? He listened to them… He should have had his head punched. He suffered vicious military dicipline and cried.

It was nearly midday when he saw a middle aged man walking with determination toward the car. The man, about average height, walked with a rolling movement that many ship deck hands adopt at sea. His stride and attitude seemed to swagger aggressively.

Vic, sensing trouble, locks the car door from within. The would be intruder grabs the door handle to wrench open the car door, he shouts "Open it up now, I've got orders from the boss to take over this car, and I don't want any mouth from you", he spoke with a hard Scottish accent. His face, fierce and determined, it was also hard and weather beaten, with scruffy red hair, greying at the sides. He had not shaved in days, and he wore an athlete's type pullover with horizontal red stripes. Altogether he looked like a rough customer. His appearance didn't frighten Vic, he'd seen, and dealt with worse men in his time. He winds down the window to speak, but the man poked his head in first, "Get out now, I'm taking the car, you understand, I'm taking over." He had alcohol on his breath, it stank.

"No!" came the command "Nothing doing buster, I'm not handing anything over to a drunken second rate ex matelot." These chosen words served to infuriate him. Hesitant in anger, he draws a small hand pistol from under his pullover, moves to aim it at his opponents head, and opens his mouth to speak. In a flash seizing the opportunity, Vic opened the car door with speed and force, it struck hard against the assailant, sending him off balance, the pistol fires in to the sky as he fell sideways to the ground. Vic was upon him before he could fully recover. As the pistol was again poised to shoot, it was speedily kicked out of his hand, and spun out of reach under the car. Jock attempts to get back upon his feet again only to have his legs kicked from under him before he could fully stand upright. His confidence shattered, he reverted to abuse of the English and Scottish language, aiming four letter words at a violent rate towards the Sassenach, Vic.

"Don't try to get up, stay there and listen" Vic ordered.

He's not used to being humiliated and sprung upon his feet to get again the same treatment, falling backward upon his arse. "Now listen, I've an important message for you to take to your boss. You are to tell him that I am not handing over this consignment to anybody except to himself, and new terms and conditions will apply. Baker's the man I deal with, not you, now get your boss here".

Whilst sitting upon the ground Jock could see his pistol under the other side of the car, he can get it! The car-park attendant heard the shot, hurried to the scene, to be grabbed and thrown into collision with Vic, the disturbance sufficient enough to allow the Scot, in a flash, to roll himself over the car bonnet, and fall near the pistol. Seeing his intent, Vic swiftly gets back into the car's driving seat and winds up the windows. Jock stands up, a little unsteady, with the pistol pointed at Vic's head. He takes on an air of superiority. In an angry Gaelic accent he said "Now

V J Tarry

I command, I'll take this car even if I have to put a hole in your head."
Making demands, his words had no effect. Vic had faced many threats at
gun point before, and this one's no different.

"You damned drunken Gaelic slob, if you fire that silly thing at me,
you will only shatter the glass screen, the bullet may go anywhere and
glass splinter could blind you.

Jock's thought processes seemed to be slow. The insulting words were
chosen for effect to distract him… Vic discreetly moved to take into his
left hand the press switch that laid between the front seats. It was connected by a long flexible cable to the suitcase in the back… Jock held
the pistol firmly in his right hand and steps clear of the kerbside door,
opening it with his left hand. Alert to any reprisal he moves stealthily
to sit upon the car seat, carefully closing the door behind his move. Vic
makes no attempt to do anything, sat calmly observing the Scot's anxious
moves. Pointing the pistol close to Vic's head, he said in a firm voice.
"Get out, leave the key in the lock and move clear of the car"

Vic looked with a smirk upon his face, dithered and worried the Scott
turned his back upon the invader and with dignity left the car, a length
of cable trailing from his hand, and the car key remaining in his pocket.
Jock eases himself into the driving seat, still holding the pistol pointing
at Vic as he moved away.

Jock yells out "You're so stupid, don't you understand that I could put
a hole in your head. This pistol is not a toy; I'm not playing games, now
come back here with the key"

"You think I'm stupid, have you noticed the cable from my hand running to the case in the back of the car. That case contains enough explosive to blow the car into smithereens. In my hand you can see I have a
small thumb press switch. A simple press and everything will be scat-
tered over a wide area. You may have noticed that I'm moving away to a
safe distance out of range of your pistol and an explosion. You however
remain sitting on a bomb and I have the trigger. Don't start tugging the
cable you won't break it, but you could set off an explosion that will tear
you into pieces. The police would swarm in here with fire crew and air
ambulances. We are equally sure that we don't want anything like that to
happen. If you're thinking that I am bluffing, let me advise you that only

67

The Lesser Evil

Mister Baker and yourself have anything to loose if the car explodes. The police will firstly suspect terrorist activities being so near an international airport. They will examine every thing and everybody; some very pertinent question will have to be answered."

The concerned worried Scotsman weighs the situation, turns to see the suitcase with cable leading from it, seeing it's out of his reach. He's not a gambling man, he is worried, also he has no key to start the engine, so he feels trapped and rather stupid.

Vic yells to him "I was a sergeant in the army; there I learnt to deal with explosives, mines, booby-traps and demolition. It would be in everybody's best interest if you give up, walk away and tell your boss about the suitcase and its contents, that I am willing to talk business and hand over the vehicle to him only on my terms. Get me a telephone number. I will talk to him. Don't take too long, it's already past my lunch time" …

He looks at the weapon in his hand, his target about 30 paces distant. If he shot at him from that distance he couldn't be sure to hit him, also he might press the button and blow up the lot as he fell. He couldn't be sure of anything, he was not sure of himself. He hesitated left the car, held his pistol in the air, and took out the cartridge case to render it ineffective, "You see that I've surrendered, I'll tell the boss you want to talk, and perhaps he'll give yer a phone line number. I'm sure he won't show up here". He was still muttering something as he sauntered away, ashamed of his own failure. Mister Baker will be furious; he will need to keep out of his way for the next few days.

Vic returns to the car, taking the length of cable with him reeling it up into small circles, and placing it conveniently by for future use. So far it has served him well, he mused… Waiting patiently for something further to happen he pondered with interest that the car park attendant had expected the car to arrive, albeit a day late, both Sladen and the Scotsman recognised the car upon sight. This particular car must have been here before perhaps more than once. He reasoned that he was not the first person to bring the car into the country. Studying his predicament, remembering the garage owner looking under the car whilst it was hoisted up for underside inspection, saying that "if you undo those four bolts the front boxed in bumper assembly would just about fall off". The

68

rear was also easily removed by undoing four similar bolts. Vic Brandon reasoned there might be many front and near bumpers in constant use all of the time.

"This car has front wheel drive" the mechanic said, further pondering the car construction to include the closing in of the tunnel along which the propeller shaft would normally run to drive the rear axle, not needed with front wheel drive. Boxing in this space would provide additional storage for a lot more contraband. He envisaged every conceivable space employed in this way by clever engineering, design bringing into use secret compartments. Each would have to have means for filling as well as emptying even if not detached from the car.

He envisages a place, perhaps an out of the way farm building, something like a barn, into which the car is taken and systematically dissembled, there would be vacuum equipment to extract the powder from the various receiver compartments. The cocaine powder being processed with other addictive substances into tablets suitable for street market consumers. It's an evil trade, carried on by evil men, damaging many lives. Vic shudders at the thought he's in possession of more than a million pounds worth of the stuff. He's getting impatient, over half an hour has passed and no sign of the messenger. A few cars come into the car park and some went out, none carried any word from Mister Baker or his stooges.

Vic's hot and impatient like waiting for the enemy to make a move. Like the jungle, heat seemed to close in around him. Lying quietly in the burning sun numerous crawling and flying insects pestered and constantly annoyed him. He hated the jungle, the steaming heat and the thick undergrowth and diseases. He was never meant to be there, never mind die there. It's a long time ago now. He laid back listening to the noises of the jungle.

The sun beaming down makes the car hot and himself sluggish. He opens the side window and the afternoon warm air breezes in… He hears the gentle whines, murmurs, screeches, yapping all around. He never expected to be penned down in a bloody stinking bog-hole in the middle of a stinking slimy jungle 6000 miles from home. Hiding in a damp smelly undergrowth of decaying vegetation, waiting to be cut to pieces by enemy bullets, and left to be food for scavengers. Oh! How he struggled to hang onto sanity…

The Lesser Evil

Vic looks out across the car parking area, the sun is blazing and everything's quiet, nobody stirs and he's thirsty… and sweating…

Smiling to himself, he wasn't so much frightened now that the Japs are quiet. You got used to anything in time and he had been fighting in this hell of a country for so many months that time didn't matter anyway. It's bloody wrong that he got used to death, blood and torn crippled bodies, yet he did in time. Now he's bloody annoyed, because they needn't have been in that bog hole, waiting to be cut to pieces by the Nips except for a madly enthusiastic silly sod of an officer who without proper military appraisal of the situation, led them into the enemies trap.

A few men had been sent out to observe the ground. They set out under a green Lieutenant with one Sergeant Brandon. The lieutenant leads 'em out into the jungle, they progressed until it thickened and they had to squeeze through every yard of the green hell. Quietness was essential. Suddenly it opened up clear again. They advanced about 150 yards before the Japs opened fire. All hell was let loose for a few minutes. The area was swarming with them. There's yelling, screaming mingled with incessant gun fire and explosions. Those not dead took cover. Brandon and two others survived by taking shelter in a green slimy wet stinking slime. Darkness soon falls in the jungle, it gave the three men the chance to escape. Grovelling and groping they were able to move like snakes away from the bog hole to safer ground. It would be a long night. The noises at times enough to set your teeth on edge. The cold sent shivers through their bones. He hated it…hated it… by dawn they were away from it.

Vic's sweating, he daren't leave the car he feared somebody watching might seize it. The feeling that he is constantly under surveillance made the hair at the back of his neck tingle. It's been a long time; he's feeling hungry and brought no sustenance with him.

"Hunger sharpens the senses", he said to himself. Looking ahead he sees the Scotsman approaching holding something in his hand above his head to make it seen.

It's a mobile radio telephone, the same type used by the army in field training. His eyes followed every move. It might be something else in his hand ready to throw at the car or himself. The radio phone was placed upon the car bonnet and the man turned away without saying a word. Careful it might be a trap.

The Scotsman was all of 30 yards away before the radio phone was taken up to Vic's ear, it had been switched on.

"Bwandon, Hello, Bwandon do you hear me Bwandon? It's Reg Baker here, over."

Vic let him call a little longer, he'd waited over an hour for this call, he's not going to appear eager now.

"Mr Bwandon do you hear me? over". With a very casual tone of voice he replied.

"To whom do you wish to speak Sir?"

"Bwandon you double crossing cheat so you've booby trapped the car and holding it for ransom. You won't get away with that stunt on me. I have ways of dealing with upstarts like you. You'll regret every move against me. You understand. I'll make you squirm" His voice got louder as he spoke obscenities.

Vic was calm and placid said, "Mister Baker, you cheated me, I'm the offended party. You set me up to bring your car into the country knowing full well that it was loaded with narcotic drugs without letting on a word of its contents. You told me nothing of the risk I was taking, believing me to be a stupid naïve Sergeant. You exploited my willingness to be co-operative. I took in and believed every word you said but I have since found out differently…"

Baker, shouting: "You were well paid in cash for what you did you bloody fraud, you agreed to deliver the car now hand it over."

"I've got the merchandise in my possession; I'm sitting on it right now. It's a very cleverly designed vehicle loaded in every concealed compartment with cocaine, the stuff's worth about two million quid street market value. I'm not handing over the drugs for the peanuts you gave me…The Traveller's cheque were no good not negotiable, no bank will take them…

There's a pause, Baker's thinking about the words he heard.

71

The Lesser Evil

"How did you find out about the drugs, who else knows about your particular errand, do the police or the customs know about this?" His voice now anxious, cautious and hesitant, he's worried.

"The police and customs know nothing about the contents of the car but 'Ken Flowers knows.'"

Baker shouts the name, "Flowers, Ken Flowers. That swindling lying bastard, have you been talking to him, how did he come into this? I've known Ken Flowers for a long time he never did anybody any favours."

"Mister Flowers said that you and he knew each other well and that he was imprisoned for your crime. Now he seeks revenge and allies! Vic said.

"All that's by the way, my interest is not Mister Flowers, police or customs. My deal is this. I have the goods that you want and I will hand over the complete consignment to you personally at a time and place that I will designate not giving more than one hour notice tomorrow in exchange for £50,000 pounds sterling in English bank notes packed in a suitable small case.

The notes I will check which will take about 10 minutes. The transaction will take place between you and I only in a wide open space where it would be difficult for any other person to approach without being seen. Thus minimising any trickery on either part. It's simple, you want the merchandise I want the money. It's a straight forward exchange."

Baker shouts: "You damned stupid fool Bwandon dictating to me about what you are going to do and you expect me to go along with your stupid fucking stunt. The car and contents are mine, I paid you for your part, now you delivered the car as agreed and that's the end of the contract. I am ordering you leave the car now because my patience is exhausted. I am not giving you any fifty thousand for it now. I'd sooner have Jimmy put a bullet through your head."

"That's his name 'Jimmy' he was here earlier threatening me with a silly little hand pistol. Neither he nor you frighten me. All of your shouting, raving and 'menacing' do not worry me. I've dealt with fiercer enemies than you. I've been a civilian less than three month and you set me up with a high risk venture bringing the drugs into the country. If I'd been caught in possession I would most likely have to serve a sentence
72

in prison whilst you would deny any knowledge of the whole business. 'I don't know the man, never met him' you'd say. The same as you did with Ken Flowers. They found the stuff secreted aboard his lorry destined for you and you denied him all the way through. Mister Flowers attempted to hijack the car at a motorway service area car park. I was able to defeat his attack and hold him in submission. He mumbled something about having read my advertisement and realised that I might be a candidate for one of your schemes.

"He waited outside my flat the morning I left. He followed my car to Southampton in order to see my face. He saw me aboard the ferry and again as I was driving the car through Dover Customs. He followed the car to the service areas where he and another attempted to hijack it. They intended to hold the car for ransom and vengeance against the man he said he knew to be Mister Reginald Lesser alias Baker. Because of your criminal activities involving me I have made a bad start in my civil life and I must rectify that. My demand for fifty thousand pounds is by way of compensation for cheating, misusing and putting me at perilous risk."

Vic could hear Lesser mumbling trying to say something as he spoke.

"Mister Lesser did you hear what I was saying to you.. There were constant interruptions from you so perhaps I'd better go over it again."

"Damn and blast you Bwandon I do not use the name Lesser. Baker's the name get used to it."

"I have no intention to get used to your name I've spelt out my demands and I wish this association to end very soon."

"Then leave the car and take your Fucking bomb with you."

"I'll willingly do that as soon as you pass the cash into my hand."

"You damned stupid fool you're asking for trouble. My patience is just about exhausted talking to you through this blasted heavy radio phone. I've had enough of you sod off."

"One more minute please, Mister Baker, If you will not take the car for my payment I have many options. I can explode the car here, near the International Airport which will cause the various authorities to investigate thinking it could be an act of Terrorism. They would find residue of drugs and a simple capped cylinder shaped tin box container in which will be each document you gave me, plus those I got from the German Court and the German Police also a statement from myself concerning what I know about this matter. Subsequently I will be interviewed, there will be questions to answer.

"The next option open to me is to negotiate with Ken Flower. I told you he went to considerable trouble to get the car from me. Another possibility I can drive the car off the quay at Poole into the bay. What the authorities will make of that, a car loaded with cocaine recovered from the sea is bound to start top level enquiries particularly with the customs people here and abroad."

"Now Mister Baker I'm sure you would not want me to take any of these actions. Look at it this way, I have no roots, no ties. I could blow the car tell the police everything they want to know, leave my flat and leave the country. You would be left to deal with the consequences. Surely it's worth giving me the cash I demand and end the matter there."

Vic could almost hear him thinking... before he said, "You're a bloody mean hard bargain driver. I've never had to deal with such a vicious, destructive, dangerous bastard like you ever before... You've gained a reputation for being a stubborn bastard among other things."

"I'm sure you know. After this slanging match can we now get to the business at hand?"

Vic's waiting in silence he could almost feel what Lesser or Baker's next words would be.

"How will I know that the proposed transaction will end the matter? Knowing what you're likely to do and what you are capable of I don't feel I can trust you. You're a devious customer Bwandon."

"We will have to trust each other. There's honour amongst thieves and the likes of us both. I need the money, you need the drugs. As I said before it's a simple business transaction: you take the car in which will be all the evidence including all the incriminating documents and you drive it away leaving me with £50,000 cash and you will not see or hear from me again, that's the deal... I can set it up early tomorrow."

"I don't think I can raise that amount of cash by tomorrow, however, I'll phone you to let you know and make arrangements to hand it over if I can manage it."

74

"No!", Vic yells out. "No, I'll phone you with details of how, where and when to avoid any misunderstanding and trickery. As for raising the money I believe drug dealers don't put their money into commercial banks to avoid it being traced to its source and to avoid tax. Therefore, I'm sure you will be able to pack sufficient notes into a small case. You must give me a contact telephone number for me to give you last minute instructions about our meeting. I advise you to have an Ordinance Survey map, Dorset Sheet No. 127, one inch to a mile. The venue will be given to you by map references and description with exact timing. It's important to be punctual I will not hang about long, delaying I fear will give you much time for reprisal. I feel in our dealing and way of talking to each other trickery and reprisal cannot be ruled out. If any retaliatory action is suspected everything will be aborted. Any attack upon me or the car and I will press the button." 'Bang.'

"You Fxxxing Shithouse of Sergeant Bwandon giving me orders as if I were one of your recruits. You're damn right there will be reprisals. Nobody uses me the way you have done without me retaliating, my time will come and I will see you squirm in anguish and suffering. But for the time being you have me at a disadvantage."

Replying with a military type voice to further annoy Lesser, Vic said, "Thank you for that epilogue, we've been through all that before now pay attention Mr Baker your ranting does not impress me. We must now get back to business. Please give me your contact telephone number for tomorrow morning. I'll phone you early to finalise a programme with specified movements. You will find your field telephone I'm using in the car when you collect it. Now if you will give me that number I wish to be away until tomorrow."

Vic Brandon noticed that every time Lesser spoke the name 'Brandon' he seemed to have difficulty voicing it saying 'Bwandon' instead, "I'll phone you in the morning at your place early about eight."

"No!… not possible I've had my phone disconnected to avert nuisance calls." This was not true but he did not want Lesser to avoid giving his telephone number there and then. "It's back to you, can I have that number?"

The Lesser Evil

Baker's reluctance to give a telephone contact indicates his resistance to co-operate. He's not going to give away a small fortune if he can avoid it. Thinking over what Jenny said that Baker will always get somebody else to do his dirty work, he might therefore give somebody else's telephone number. Vic's never seen Mister Baker, how will he recognise him? Jenny's description was adequate enough to build a mental picture of him, but to be sure further and better details are necessary. Lesser's speech imediment will identify him.

"Mister Baker, we can get no further without your number."

There was no response from the other end. Vic suddenly thought that all citizen band radio phones must be registered with the General Post Office for telephone numbers and licence.

"Mister Baker, hello, I've just thought that all walky talky phones must be registered with the post office and I have one in my hand through which we communicate. I can request your number simply by dialling directory enquiries… If we are using illegal equipment the G.P.O. will seek details. Perhaps it would be less troublesome to give me your regular contact number?"

"Bwandon, I've underestimated you. You're a cunning rotten swine", now he's modifying his language a little, a persistent one at that…"

"Tomorrow morning I'll be at the farm about 9 o'clock you can call me there. Mister Boothe will answer; he will call me to the office we can talk privately. The number, listen carefully I'll not repeat it."

Vic writes every digit in the correct order in the palm of his hand.

"Thank you I've got it, call you sharp at 9 tomorrow, over and out."

Within a few minute Vic Brandon's driving away from the Southampton car park, but is not sure that other cars following are friend or foe. He leaves the main road by suddenly jerking the car into a housing estate, steering left and turning right to discover another exit. He was sure no body followed that manoeuvre… Driving towards Wareham he remembered Harry his good friend from the Army life. Harry secured employment as a farm manager upon a big estate with a house thrown in. He should be so lucky. He had invited Vic to come to the farm any time he wished to make a phone call to arrange a visit. Now's the time for that call he mused. Parking the car outside a small Forest Inn on route through to Wareham he enters to get a beer and a sandwich. Sitting himself by a window so that he could see the car he finalises his plan. He swallowed the last of his beer. He used the payphone in the foyer to speak to his friend Harry. It was agreed that they could meet at the farm. He phoned his partner, Jenny but spoke to John Hardwick and gave him an update upon events so far.

"Please tell Jenny that I hope she will agree to a business dinner again at The Commodore restaurant tonight at 8 o'clock."

Later in the afternoon Vic passes over the railway level crossing nearby the Wareham railway station and drove on towards Sandford. A farm service gravelled track leads from the main road to the right. Along this track about 600 yards he crosses over a single lane farm service bridge over a railway to enter a very large area of open meadow recently cleared of its hay crop now with only golden straw stubble. The gravelled way continues through this field meandering much further on to the farm house unseen in the distance behind a high hedge. At a point where the track is banked up about 2 feet upon either side. He surveys the area and stops the car in the middle of the field and gets out of the vehicle. Opening up an ordinance survey map upon the car bonnet, he finds his exact location with a six figure map reference. Crossing the railway bridge is the only way in to and out of this farm by vehicle. From his standpoint he can see everything crossing that bridge over 500 paces distant. To the north about 300 paces is a railway cutting with high wire mesh fence. To the south trees and scrub down to a farmhouse and a river bank. Vic sees this spot as an ideal rendezvous with all round good vision and most importantly, restricted access.

This will be where the meeting and exchange will take place tomorrow. He stands silently looking around taking in the peace and quiet until a train rumbled along the railway line disturbed the absolute stillness of the place. He hadn't seen Harry in more than two years when he attended his farewell party following many years of exemplary military service. Upon meeting, now both civilians, they hugged each other as comrades do chatting about the good times and the bad times together. Harry was most interested to learn what use Vic intended to make of the hayfield, wishing him the best of luck. Regretting that he could not in anyway give assistance as he would be working in a field about four miles away that day. They drank bottles of beer between themselves for old times sake and the usual parting of old pals. Vic's satisfied with his plans and is eager to be telling Jenny, his team mate, all about it at dinner. He drove the valuable car to Poole town railway Station and parked it in a nearby covered car park, upon entry he collects a ticket from a machine. A fee is payable before the car is taken through the exit barrier. Vic is satisfied the car will be safe there overnight.

He walks to the town's main shopping centre and buys an exquisite French perfume: gift wrapped; for the lady at his table that night.

"This is a lovely alluring and expensive perfume, may I presume it's for a special lady?", the pretty sales girl asked. She'd been well trained. He agreed, "She is very special." He had never previously bought perfume or a gift for any lady before, a feeling of benevolence and self assured confidence overcame him. She will love it.

Jenny was frequently on his mind, from the moment their eyes first met he knew there and then that they would meet again, he intends that to be recurring.

It was late in the afternoon when he stepped from the bus opposite the dwelling. He walked up to his flat on the fourth floor without meeting anybody on the way in. He makes himself a coffee, starts to undress and the telephone rings. 'Lesser', he thought checking up on him. He'd told him the phone was disconnected. He let it ring again, then lifted the receiver.

"Vic" she said in an anxious voice. "It's Jenny here. I'm dying to know what happened, John told me you were shot at. Are you alright?" her voice full of anxiety and concern for him more than would be expected of a mere business partner.

"Jenny, of course I'm alright. It's lovely to hear your voice. I've had to deal with a couple of vulgar, violent men with harsh threatening voices today so yours, is like music to my ears. I'll give you a full account tonight at dinner. I have a few questions to ask you, to clear up doubts in my mind. Also please book the table again for us both. By the way I'll be in a taxi calling to pick you up at quarter to eight at your place if that's alright?"

"Yes, I'll be ready on time and book our table. I'm eager to hear all about how you've got on today and the plans, or should I say the scheme you will employ tomorrow. See you later. Goodbye!" Her voice so affectionate, so sympathetic, it lifted his ego a lot.

He hops into the shower, scrubs up, shaves and grooms himself for his lady at table. The previous evening she turned out looking perfectly charming and he's going to be equally charming perhaps after dinner she will let him through the door. Whilst dressing for the evening he finds himself humming a newly released popular tune. It's one of those songs that get stuck in one's mind, 'Strangers in the Night'. He dismisses it to attend to his dress as best he could. He had not been able to get together a suitable civilian wardrobe relying upon the one and only suit he bought since leaving the army. He has designs to be a smart well dressed, well spoken man.

He tidies a few things away, whilst considering his plan to hand over the car load of drugs. Thoughts dash in his mind, he must be in position a long time before Lesser is scheduled to arrive. He must recheck everything and review the environment immediately he has told Lesser the venue for their meeting and he must inform John Hardwick who plans to be ready with the helicopter to move in.

Although his plan is clear in his mind he has doubts and misgivings. He knows exactly what he's going to do... He does not know enough about Mister Baker, (alias Lesser) to be able to assess in any way what he might, at this moment be planning to do, if, and when, a meeting takes place. An urgent thought stabs his mind. Lesser knows where he's living somebody could storm into his flat and take him by force holding him for ransom, his life in exchange for the car load of drugs, he could be beaten up and lucky to survive alive. Further thoughts directed his mind to the possibility that the next morning when he leaves his dwelling to collect the car he could be followed to the car park and attacked before entering the car.

There's nothing to be done about that now, he said to himself and directed his thought again to meeting Jenny for dinner. He is wondering exactly when he will give her the present of perfume. Perhaps after the dessert course would be the most effective time.

The Lesser Evil

When the taxi arrived to pick up Jenny, Vic is sitting in the back. The journey is about 15 minutes and he expected to be alone with her for that time. He is aware of feeling encouraged, excited, even passionate in her company and wishing to find the opportunity to tell her whilst they are alone in the cab. In the restaurant it will be mostly business and no likely opportunity for romantic chatting.

She enters the cab beside him and they kiss not affectionate more by way of greeting. She tells the tax driver, "The Commodore please." The cab moves swiftly through the evening traffic. Her eyes light up with a smile upon her lips. She is pleased that he sustained no wound. Jenny demanded to know about the pistol shooting maniac and about the fake bomb in the car. She began to see her man as a courageous hero and she is excited by his defiance of the gunman.

The cab arrived at the restaurant quicker than he anticipated. Soon after they had settled at their table with a meal in front of them both, she overwhelmed him by her eagerness to know everything, giving him no opportunity to romance her.

They sat at the same table they occupied the previous evening. Vic noticed that she had done her hair rather specially nice and he said so to her. Smiling in response to his compliment she said "I'm pleased you like it that's a new style for me." She moved the conversation on to seek more details of his adventures. Complements were out of place just then.

During their meal she frequently asked questions and got many answers. He watched her eyes and facial expressions. Although she was tense with anxiety she was radiant with it and took in every word said.

Jenny, keen to co-operate and be helpful went through every details of the intended scheme to trap Baker into taking the car load of drugs. Her fear is expressed in her anxious faltering voice: she said,

"I cannot but feel that you are taking dangerously high risks, you have been given Baker's reputation for treachery and trickery and he makes his own rules to suit his game. Although you have chosen the field your enemy will choose the weapons, when and how to use them. He could simply just drive into the field and shoot you dead. Yes he'd have to call your bluff to do so. That might be a risk he would take."

"Jenny, I remember you saying that Baker was not a gambling man and that he will always get somebody else to take the risk and do his dirty work for him. Tomorrow, I expect to meet Mister Baker, but as you know he's a stranger to me. I have only listened to his aggressively hard voice over a telephone and of course I have your description of him and his character. Is there any other personal details that you can remember about this man?"

It was a futile thing to ask of her, she was so engrossed and emotionally involved in the drama, thinking did not come clear. It's firmly in his mind all that she previously told him about Mister Baker and that image will have to suffice for the time being.

Vic then gave her an account of his intended programme for the next day, explaining that she can take no direct part in it.

"If all goes as planned the scheme will be over and done with by 11.30 hours. And I could be holding more money than I have ever had. Baker will be driving away the car, the monitor sending out signals and the chase will commence."

Jenny just stared, shrugged her shoulders and said in a lame voice, "Oh! How I hope so."

Turning their attention to their dinner the dessert dishes being placed in front of them, being asked by the waiter if he should replenish their drinks. They smiled pleasantly to each other and agreed one more drink. She a Martini, he a Brandy dry ginger ale. This was a good time to change their conversation. She stood up apologised and walked to the ladies room. He sat down, his eyes followed her every movement. She had a lovely correct figure and moved her long legs gracefully. He watched her every step as she adroitly returned to the table, her chair being positioned for her as she sat. He placed a small parcel upon the table in front of her. It delighted his eyes to see her expression upon loosening the pretty bow and wrapping and take out the presentation box a spray of well know French perfume. Her face lit up with gratitude she had accepted the present with all her heart. She knows that it's expensive and that he must have spent his last few pounds buying it for her. She reached out to him across the table, took his hand pressing it firmly in recognition of his affection and gift.

81

The Lesser Evil

"How did you know this is my favourite perfume?", she asked with a quizzical expression on her face.

"A few days ago when you were attending the court in Düsseldorf, you unaware, turned nearly colliding with me. Two of my senses were aroused: your attractive eyes fascinated me and your perfume disturbed me. It did it again last night when I was close to you, so I remembered it. I think I shall have your scent with me for ever"

"You say the loveliest things. Thank you." She accepted his gift.

"When you left the table a couple of thoughts went through my mind. Yesterday as I sat here, at this table in the evening, you were telling me about your rather traumatic experience in Italy. Mark the newspaper reporter was able to obtain for your enquiry two telephone numbers from the hotel Vigliana to England. One number you recognised as your own the other number John said he would find out who answers to that particular number. Do you know whether he did get any response?"

"Yes, John told me a few days later that it turned out to be a public call telephone box in north Dorset." Those few words started alarm bells ringing. North Dorset: Baker's farm house is in the Veracity Farm Complex of North Dorset. Vic was given Lesser's contact telephone number that same day and wrote it in the palm of his hand with a ball point pen. Later it was entered into his notebook.

Jenny said she remembers the first three numbers were her birth date 30th July or 307. Vic looked into his hand. He could still faintly see the numbers he had written 30741. Turning to meet her curiosity he showed her his palm.

"Does that look like the number?", he asked. She studies the paint figures on his palm.

"Yes, I think it is. It's nearly 2 years ago but I am sure about the first three numbers, the other could be. The whole number could be the same as was given to me by Mark in Italy. I can check it out later. The note with both numbers on it is in my briefcase at the flat." When she seemed to be on the edge of discovering something her face lights up. She needs to look into her briefcase to confirm the telephone number. Seeing curiosity on his face. She said, "Vic I'll phone you first thing tomorrow morning with the correct telephone numbers."

82

"No, I'll not be in my place tonight nor tomorrow morning. I'll have to take every precaution now, Lesser knows where I live. He or somebody could wait in hiding for me to leave my flat, follow me to where I have parked the car, over power me and take possession of it leaving me seriously injured. No! I'm dictating the policy now. I'm sure Lesser will not like it. Tomorrow at about 11am I'll expect Lesser to arrive to complete the deal. He will get the venue and instructions from me over the telephone, not more than 1 hour beforehand. I'll expect he will live up to his reputation, to avoid handing over any cash to me. He might bring in any number of dirty tricks and I'll have to use my initiative and instincts to deal with whatever he throws at me."

Jenny stared with a feared expression on her face, her lips drawn tight. She takes in a deep breathy releasing the tension in her body and mind. Perhaps she cared for him more than she realised. For a moment she wasn't sure what to say. He's not going back to his flat for his own safety. Should she offer to share her accommodation with him. That's what she thought he was expecting her to do. The instant Jenny was about to make a suggestion he said "and of course I'll be sleeping in the car tonight it will give me solitude and time to think."

"You can't sleep all night in the car, you won't get any proper rest. You'll need to be fit and alert tomorrow. I can fix you up with something better and more comfortable, stay with me."

She said those words upon impulse but they were in the back of her mind.

"That's a great offer under any other circumstance I'd jump at it."

Hesitating before saying anything further. He thought of the previous evening when she politely declined to let him enter her flat. There are occasions when a woman is not ready to take a lover into her life. She was relieved if not a little surprised when Vic adamantly said, "I've made up my mind, it's the car for me tonight. You might guess this will not be a new experience for me."

"What will you do for breakfast in the morning... shall I make you something to take with you?"

"You're a darling for being so concerned about me. I'll get something as I pass the railway station yard. There's an all-night coffee stall there, patronised by many long distance lorry drivers and travellers. I'm sure I'll get something to tied me over until lunch time."

She smiled briefly at his words. Jenny was not only disappointed in herself but wished she was somebody else entirely a tear glistened in her eye. She felt so mean, she reached out taking his hand she understood

"Will you have another drink, a sort of night cap?" he asked

"I'd love another Martini, you have another too it will cheer us up."

The waiter placed their drinks upon the table. He looks at Jenny, "Shall I call for a taxi soon."

"Yes, I'd like to leave after our drinks." She said forcing a smile. He returns her look and they both grinned scornful of their situation.

"Hello Jenny", she jerked her head over her shoulder to see Simon Sinclair a customs officer and colleague. Before she could respond, Simon asked "and who's your new friend?" They both stand to greet Simon. Jenny introduces Vic Brandon and they chat in a friendly manner for a few minutes. Jenny politely made it apparent that she didn't want his company longer than necessary and he soon moved on. Vic could see in her attitude that she didn't particularly like Simon Sinclair. He was out of ear shot when Jenny said, "He fancies himself a smart dick, he is divorced and he often attempted to date me. I always found some excuse which made us both uncomfortable. He's a nice enough man, but there was something about him I didn't like."

"Your cab has arrived, Sir."

In the cab he draws her close putting his arm around her whilst she nestles into his hold pressing her head upon his shoulder. She lifted her face to his, their lips meet in a passionate lingering kiss... Vic wondered about Simon Sinclair, smart, good looking ex naval office, well groomed, good manners, a too good to be true type. For the first time in his life he is jealous of another man but he could not dislike him, neither could he explain his own feeling. Their cab draws up to the entrance where Jenny lives. He takes her arm to escort her to the door. The porch entrance is flooded in soft moonlight. He turns her to face the moon, she looked at him in a wondrous gaze,

"Moonlight becomes you it's shining in your hair." Vic said.

84

Her eyes glistened, her beautifully formed moist lips reflect tinges of silver light. There's a coolness in the air, Jenny's eyes stared into his at that moment they instinctively knew they were meant for each other. He drew her closer to himself. She yielded her heart and soul to him and she melted into his arms… Their lips blended committing each to the other. Passion rises within him but not sufficient to overcome his instilled sense of duty to his self designated task. Sensual lovers feel each others anxiety and frustration, parting at that particular moment was but sweet sorrow. With a lump in his heart he remained to see her enter the building. She looked at him with considerable misgivings, sighed and said,

"Good luck tomorrow… Sleep well…" She then turns and quickly kissed him and skipped inside the door.

The moon shone brighter as he walked more like marching full of confidence along the deserted streets to the parked car which will be his lodging for the night. He had to be especially sure of himself for the morrow and the night air helped him think clearly about his encounter with Lesser and his future with Jenny…

It was about five when he awoke. It seemed only a few minutes since he'd fallen asleep. He left the car, stood to exercise and ease his limbs and his mind… This is the morning of the day that could change future events drastically for him. As in all conflicts one is only able to surmise what the opposition may be scheming to do. Considering Lesser's reputation for trickery he recalls people saying 'All's fair in love and war'. In his solitude he's aware that he is experiencing strong feelings about Jenny. Emotion akin to love which he has never previously known. There were woman in his past, they excited him and likewise he gave them equal pleasure. He never supposed himself to have been in love with anyone of them. They are no more than ghosts of the past.

He tries to fix his mind upon the task ahead. He switches his monitor device on and checks the same device hidden in the car. He expects to receive a case/parcel of money in exchange for the car contraband. His inner senses tell him that his adversary will do anything necessary to get possession of the drugs and the car. Vic Brandon will have to use all his fieldcraft, all his senses, cunning and initiative to walk away unscathed, with the cash from this challenge.

The Lesser Evil

He reminds himself that the prime purpose of the exchange is to get the car into Lesser's own hands and then to follow the signal emitted from the car to its destination. If of course money changes hands he will feel justified in keeping it by way of compensation. The words, "If we don't get Lesser we've still got you", echo in his head. He's in a predicament which will drive him on to its conclusion. Even if he wanted to there'd be no way out for him now.

He smiles contemptuously intending to win through at all costs. This is just another challenge

Looking around the parking area, nobody nothing to be seen. Quietly he drives out into the road on toward the railway station to get a coffee and an egg & bacon sandwich, which might be his last breakfast.

The Lesser Evil

FIELD TACTICS

The late summer sun burnt through the intervals in the clouded sky. Vic Brandon drove the Estate car into the field where he intends to get Lesser to meet him at precisely 11 o'clock. Looking at his watch it's 9.30. He re-iterates his plan to hand over the car contraband. Walking the perimeter of the field with binoculars slung from around his neck, starting from the entrance bridge over the railway, he shuffles slowly meandering and walking in a clockwise direction around the area. He checks every bush, tree and fold in the ground for possible places from which a supposed assault may come. He covers the ground meticulously completing the circuit. Standing in the centre of the railway bridge raising his field glasses looking east towards the car placed centrally in the field. He's satisfied that he will see everything approaching the car from the only direction it may come, over the railway bridge.

He listens to the stillness of the place. His ears straining to pick up remote sounds. The fresh wind whispers through the distant shrubbery and trees. He's keenly aware of everything around and above him. The stage is set. It's almost 10 o'clock and time to make the promised phone call. He takes up the walky-talky field telephone switches it on and dials the numbers that Lesser gave him... It responds... something like ringing at the other end...

"Hello.

"It's Vic Brandon here I have to speak to Mr Lesser please."

The Lesser Evil

A coarse male voice hesitant said, "Perhaps you want Mr Baker, you're Mr Brandon, he said you would call. He has your phone call number and will call you back immediately."

Vic was impatiently waiting it seemed like along time, perhaps it was no more than a few minutes.

Holding the phone in his hand he felt it vibrate before it made a sound, as if the bell was cracked, it just clattered.

Pressing the receive tab he said, "Brandon here. Over."

"Baker at this end ready to get your instructions. Over." Surprised, he didn't have that usual aggressive tone of voice. Previously he spoke with a commanding bullying attitude but now he's almost mellow and polite. It's Lesser alright, he recognises his voice, he's heard all the harsh tones before. Vic's disturbed... The voice change means he's smugly contemptuous of Vic's planed rendezvous. Lesser must have schemed up some stunt, a dirty trick or sudden attack. He desperately wants the drugs and might do anything to get the loaded car, not stopping at murder.

"Brandon here ready to give directions. Have your Dorset map ready." Vic Brandon reads out a map reference number.

"You start at Wareham railway station level crossing: travel the road A365 towards Poole. Exactly 2 miles along the road dips a little, about 100 yards further on to your right there's an entrance to a gravel lane with a signpost Homerton Farm. Take this lane for about half a mile you will come to an iron construction railway bridge with wooden decking. This bridge is suitable for farm traffic only. It's wide enough for one vehicle to cross at a time and is the only access to the farm and an open spacious field, the map reference which I have just given you brings you to this spot. Standing upon the bridge you will see at a distance the estate car for which you've come. The car will be positioned in the centre of a very big open area. You will also see me standing at about 35 yards away with a flexible cable leading to your car, with a detonator switch in my hand ready to explode everything if I suspect any dirty tricks. This is a straightforward transaction. You leave the parcel of money within the vehicle in which you arrive. You drive away the contraband car in which you will find every one of the incriminating documents you gave me, you will have all the evidence. I am assured that for the duration of our business we will not likely be disturbed. I'll expect you to cross the railway bridge at 11 o'clock precisely. It's now 10.15 don't be late I'm not a patient man. Over."

"Bwandon!", he shouts, "I'm a long way from Wareham it may not be possible to get to you in your set time. It might take another fifteen minutes. Over."

Vic noted the way he said his name 'Bwandon'. It's Lesser alright.

"No, you must make every effort to get to the farm on time. I'm not allowing any time for reprisals. I'll be standing watching the bridge through my field glasses at exactly 11 o'clock expecting you to arrive. Over and out."

That's it, he said to himself with fear and great emptiness in his stomach. He wished he had taken the flask of coffee that Jenny offered, he could do with it now. Vic reflects: he hates traps yet the situation in which he set himself is something similar to a trap, there's only one way out should that snap closed he'd be in peril. What could go wrong? It's impossible to imagine. Soldier's law, 'Always secure your exit.' No matter what situation you get into make sure there's a way out.

It was quiet and he immediately sensed a foreboding of disaster, a sixth sense troubled his mind. He'd never experienced anything quite like it before. He's vulnerable standing entirely alone in the emptiness of a big field. Looking up at the sky he sees ominous dark clouds forming. There's a fresh wind blowing from behind himself up the field towards the bridge. He would have liked it better had the wind blown towards him carrying every slight sound with it. As the clouds drifted along a few spots of rain fell. He'd hoped that no more would follow but it did. The wind recedes a little and his ears pick up the distant sound of a vehicle grinding its way along a gravelled track. There is one such track and that's the other side of the bridge. Vic takes up his intended position at the end of the 35 yards long cable with switch in his hand ready for any eventuality. A quick glance at his watch, it's 10:54. Lesser's early. The sound is getting closer the vehicle stops upon the up slope of the bridge and not seen nor heard by Vic's keen senses, he's puzzled. Perhaps Lesser's making sure before entering the narrow bridge, he's checking his bearings and map references. A few minutes delay, anxiety builds.

The Lesser Evil

He switches on his signal device. The vehicle moves to the parapet of the downside and stops again. Vic Brandon can now clearly see through his binoculars. It's a farm type Land Rover without a canopy over the front seats the rear half is hooded. The windscreen seems wet makes it difficult to see, but it appears that two people are seated in the front. 'Why would Lesser bring along another person?' Surely he needs no helper or witness. He immediately adjusts the field glasses focuses to get a sharper image. Every detail of the Land Rover became clear but he can't see through the glass windscreen at that peculiar higher angle, he gets only a reflection of the sky. What's he going to do? The Rover moves slowly down from the bridge turns to enter the path leading to the coveted car. It stops about 50 paces short of the estate car which Lesser so much desires. Both persons remain seated whilst he surveys the ground and the area in particular. Vic Brandon, standing defiant with the control switch in his hand does not appear to worry Lesser who's playing a waiting game hoping Vic Brandon will become nervous and make a foolish move. It seemed like a minute or two both men not speaking in a stalemate situation. Lesser sitting and staring at Brandon, Brandon curious about the other person sitting in the Land Rover on Lesser's left side appears to have his head covered.

"What stunt's Lesser intending to pull off this time?" He's about to find out. With speed and skill Lesser snatches the wet paper bag covering the other person's head and stand upright his left hand dragging that person's arm above his head in so doing causing them both to stand in full view.

Vic Brandon is flabbergasted. Lesser has handcuffed a woman to his left wrist. She had a gag cloth stuck across her mouth, distorting her face, her hair is dishevelled. Vic, in perplexed anxiety lifts and adjusts his binoculars to set a better image. He's shocked and bewildered at the same time enraged. It's Jenny. That evil swine's got Jenny. His head swims in doubt, anger and puzzlement. He sees her eyes pleading to be released from her captor. Vic's urged to liberate her. How could that swine know of his affection for Jenny? He would do anything to protect her from this evil man.

Lesser standing defiant making it very obvious that Jenny's captive to himself by handcuff. He yells against the wind.

90

V J Tarry

"Bwandon, you see I've got your queen. I have what you want; you've got what I want. She's in no way harmed although a little disturbed being used in our trading." Vic is seething with anger, he's powerless to move. Frustration is almost choking him, he wants to scream out but cannot, he's tongue tied and choking.

"Listen this is the deal now; I'll spell it out to you. Follow my instructions correctly and your woman will be released into your arms unhurt. Shout it out you understand that."

"OK you promise in no way to hurt her and I'll surrender to your demands."

"I've given you my promise. Now act as I say", Vic Brandon has no faith in his promise. He'll just have to accept that Jenny will be freed.

"Firstly take that explosive device out of my car and move it a safe distance away over there", pointing to his far right. "Disconnect your control cable and switch."

Before dropping his binoculars from hanging around his neck he looked at Jenny. Her eyes told him the nod of her head told him to do everything Lesser commands. Soon the case and detonator is placed at a safe distance out of reach.

"Get into my car and drive it around in a complete figure of eight stopping about 3 yards away from and alongside this Land Rover facing towards the bridge... Do not switch off the engine."

Vic carries out the driving manoeuvre whiles his commander and Jenny watch every turn of the wheel. Lesser assures himself that the car is not booby trapped and safe to drive away. Feeling smugly confident his evil eyes watching every move he orders Vic to perform.

"All the documents I gave you and others you collected from the Court and the police you will place upon the passenger seat along with my walky talky telephone. Get out of the car and walk about 30 yards away, not near your bomb and wait." Vic, feeling hopelessly incompetent stands at a distant seeing Jenny being pushed around unable to utter a word of protest she must go where her captor goes. Reluctantly she moves with Lesser to enter the estate car being shoved across the front seats to the passenger side. "Pick up all those papers, the phone and hold them upon your lap", he orders. Jenny studying Lesser's face, he's not the man she once knew. This monster's a vicious man with evil eyes and a tyrannical compulsion. He'll do murder to get the car full of drugs into his possession. He feverishly orders her to present each incriminating document in turn for him to approve nervously she obeys. Vic Brandon's standing at a distance in the rain seeing little of what is happening, knowing less of what Lesser's intending. He's tempted to rush at the car to liberate Jenny. He's confident that he could overpower Lesser in a fair combat but could not risk harming Jenny in anyway. He looks at the Land Rover now unattended getting ideas about seizing and driving it to block the bridge exit. Suddenly the estate car with Jenny moves forward towards the bridge. The lying swine, promised to release Jenny. Vic Brandon in panic leaps into action, running madly in the rain to the accelerating car. He's no match for the vehicle speeding away. He stops in forlorn despair, his heart sinks, his pulse racing. He's lost her. He's lost everything. He's hopelessly defeated...

The bridge decking grumbles against the car speeding over it. The gravel on the downside grinds in disarray as the car skids to a halt. Lesser is safe with his hoard over the watershed he has no further use for Jenny. In a fluster he releases himself from her ordering her and pushing her clumsily out of the car, she falls heavily upon the weeded grass verge. The car wheels spin noisily throwing up dirt and mud as it disappears down the gravel lane. Vic Brandon throws his head from side to side straining to receive and understand the sounds he gets when the car stopped and moved on again...

Jenny springs to her feet and attempts to remove the adhesive gagging tape stuck across her face. She knows that it must come off in one quick swipe otherwise it would be tediously painful. Firmly gripping one corner, her action is swift she rips the material away, a small piece of skin from her lower lip is torn away with it. Before she could feels its effect she yells against the wind and rain, "Vic I'm safe", and she runs back over the bridge. Delighted to be freed she continues yelling, "I'm safe, I'm free... of him". Lessers taken the car and taken the bait he's hooked. Victor Brandon hears her cry, his heart swells. He's compelled to run toward her he must open his heart and arms to her. "Jenny I'm coming." He quickens his pace to meet her. Jenny stumbling down the bridge ramp

92

slope with ever faltering strides she leaps falling straight into his arms. He drew her ever closer to himself. She surrenders to his loving embrace he attempted to kiss her. She put her hand to her sore lips to stop him. He then saw she was crying. "I'd love you to kiss me but it would hurt us both. As for my tears they're tears of relief, love and joy"... Vic Brandon laughed hysterically, releasing his pent up anxiety and nervous tension. His head was reeling with questions about her being taken and used by Lesser in bargaining but not now. She's safe in his arms... Hearing in the distant sky the sounds like distant thunder it's a helicopter he turns from Jenny, throws his head back, lifts his binoculars to focus upon it. Suddenly the binocular explodes in his face, the force nearly turned him round. Blood is on his left hand. He'd been shot at by a sniper intending to put a bullet through his head. Vic knows when he's been sniped. It's not a new experience. He also knows that his assailant must be laying in or along the railway cutting. His eyes turned quickly to that direction he grabbed Jenny and they fell to the ground together in the throes of death.

"Keep your head down", he said. "There's somebody out there aiming to shoot a hole in my head." The aimed bullet was just wide of the mark, they lay quiet... "Oh dear, you're bleeding." She whispered, looking at a cut above his eyebrow. "It's bleeding a lot", she said in a sad worried voice.

"Don't move the sniper might try again."

Jenny, charged with fear and anxiety feels compelled to say: "Lesser stopped the Land Rover just before crossing the bridge, a person got out of the back and without a word being said vanished. He must be the sniper out there, somewhere."

"You're right, Lesser wants to leave nobody to testify against him. That's why he released you, we're supposed to die together. His rifleman out there was to make sure of that", he said with deep concern and anger in every fibre of his body. He turned his head, it hurt like hell, blood and rain ran into his right eye, but seeing the helicopter coming in just above the trees his pain is for the moment wiped away...

The sniper confident that he'd hit his target, is worried by the chopper closing in and hovering above. Avoiding being seen he runs to the cover of the few nearby oak trees. He intends to make his way to the

Land Rover standing in the field about 50 running paces further on and there with escape the field. Vic Brandon springs to his feet lifting Jenny to hers. They both wave to the chopper which is landing a safe distance away from the railway track and into the centre field. Vic and Jenny move with their heads down toward the machine. Blood flowed form Vic's head wound and from a torn finger flesh burn leaving a trail of spots behind him. He helped Jenny into the machine and climbed inside himself to receive first aid treatment from the aircraft's medical kit and Jenny's expert hand. The engine revs up again and the chopper lifts into the sky. John Hardwick greets them both expressing bewilderment about Jenny's presence in the field. How did she get there, what is she doing here? Now is not the time for questions. The pilot soon picks up the signal emitted from the estate car being driven by Lesser toward northern Dorset.

"That's very good we have Lesser in the possession of the drugs now", said John. He looked at Vic blood seeping through the head bandage.

"We'll have that seen to immediately we land." His eyes turn to Jenny seeing the manacle on her wrist said, "and my dear you're looking as if you've been roughened up a bit too. And by the way congratulations to both of you." That's all there's likely to get for the time being. "Mr Lesser will be arrested and charged with offences in connection with drug dealing. The Police have been alerted and I'll be giving them 'action stations' straightaway."

He takes the headgear from the pilot, the radio previously turned to the police headquarters and said:- code word "Egor" and spells it out "EGOR". John Hardwick knows that two police cars are poised ready to receive and follow instant instructions from himself in the surveillance helicopter.

Down on the ground the sniper believed to be the Scottish Matelot Jimmy, sees the chopper climbing in the distance and feels safe to break cover. He saw his targets Vic and Jenny climb into the helicopter. Disappointed at his own performance with a rifle, blaming the wind, the rain and target movement. He hurriedly throws the rifle into the back of the Land Rover as he comes up to it from behind… He sees the key left in the starter switch presumably for him to make his get away. Jimmy wipes the rain from the seat with his left forearm sleeve, sits upon the seat and

94

turns the key. An almighty explosion instantly rips the vehicle into fragments and Jimmy left this earth in a violent disarray. The noise shattered the peace of the field and birds in panic took flight. The occupiers of the helicopter heard and saw the explosion shortly before they felt the blast of it. Looking out black smoke is towering into the sky with big pieces of the torn apart vehicle rocketing upward and outward, from the ground where once stood the Land Rover. They all looked in silent horror at the malicious act. The vehicle had been prepared and set to destroy whoever should turn the key. John Hardwick, an ex Navel Commander had seen many explosion, seen many good men die fighting for their country, the freedom of the seas and their loved one's. This explosion is tragically different, the work of a sick and evil mind in the service of the devil.

The chopper's radio responds with the code word "EGOR". Dorset Police "You are surveying a vehicle seen from your position in the helicopter. We have previously received descriptions of the vehicle and will pick it out and follow at a safe discreet distance according to your directions. Sergeant Mullet of the Northern Area is tuned into your signal waiting with two cars and two constables in each car to close into the place where Lesser's car is destined." The radio contact is left open. Vic Brandon and John study an ordinance survey detailed map of the ground under them making it easier to follow the car and predict the route Lesser's intending. Vic removes the wreckage of the binoculars still hanging around his neck, looking close into it he quaked at the destruction the rifle bullet made. It was to have been his head! Suddenly a sharp piercing pain shot through his wound making him feel sick to his stomach.

"Ah."

Jenny watching with concern at the blood still seeping into his head bandage asked, "Vic, are you all right?"

"Yes, I'll be fine in a minute." He put up a brave face as he said it. "I've suffered worse than this", he said patting his head bandage and transferring blood to his fingers. John Hardwick, following the cars movement on the ground, said over the radio, "He's driving the car along the A325 route now toward Rigby. This could be the road to enter Veracity farm where Lesser has his country house residence and we suspect a drug processing factory will also be found there."

The Lesser Evil

Following about a half mile behind Lesser's car the police car in the north area came in to say they know where the farm is and they are not more than 4 or 5 miles away from the place.

Looking down from the sky they saw the contraband car entering the farm. Mr Lesser had no reason to suspect his car had been plotted and followed. The car drove along the private road to enter the farm yard premises, Hardwick alerted both police cars to close in. He advised the pilot to get in a position lower and over a suitable near by field onto which he could land the machine giving easiest possible access to the farm house.

The target car moves steadily along the lane for about half a mile in from the road, a spacious turnaround area the centre of which there stands a large obsolete agricultural machine, something like a centre-piece. The car moves around this, goes off to the right where there is built a big storage barn. The great oak doors open, the car drives straight into the building and the doors automatically close behind it. It's safe inside… Jenny's sharp eyes notice that there is a well worn foot path from the side entrance of the barn to the side of the Farm house. She thought this showed that much human activity took place between these two build-ings. The aerial view showed up more details as the helicopter descents. The house roof covered a large spacious farmhouse type residence with many bedrooms. To the north side were seen a long hutted type chalet. The house front entrance with double opening doors was approached over two wide steps covered with an ornate architraved porch. The back garden, mostly a well kept lawn exceeds to a rear path and a maintenance workshop. A light weight truck, often use in the building trade, is parked near by… Lesser steps out from the barn side door and is shocked to see the chopper making to land a short distance off in the field. Unreasoning fear seizes his mind, he runs full pelt in panic to the house, noticing two police cars coming down the drive. He enters the house in a frenzy, the police are bound to find drug processing equipments, thousands of ready made illegal tablets ready to be dispatched to the street markets, he's trapped. The helicopter puts down about 50 yards from the farm house side entrance. Lesser locks the door behind himself, rushes about like a maniac to secure every other door and window. John Hardwick and Vic

96

hurriedly leave the helicopter to meet the police advising two constables to take possession of the barn and its contents. Police Sergeant Mullet speedily drove the police car around the centre piece to stop half facing the House front entrance. The other police car about 30 yards behind facing the barn entrance doors. John Hardwick came to advise the Sergeant that perhaps Lesser had barricaded himself in the house and that he could be dangerous. Whilst the Sergeant, John and Vic stood looking at the house, weighing up the situation, surveying the possible means of approach, Jenny appeared standing confidently by Vic's side. Her presence and her safety were of immediate concern to the Sergeant who ordered her to sit in the back of the police car, there being no better place available at that moment. She would have much preferred to be with the men. Reluctantly she settled in to the rear of the car watching every move in anticipation. Vic, also concerned, turned smiling his approval of Jenny's co-operation, her eyes shine toward Vic in response. Sergeant Mullet takes from the car a handheld loudhailer ready to warn the house occupiers of the police presence… Suddenly a shot rings out, harsh male voices intermingled with female screeches screamed out from within. Men brawling like wild animals tearing at each other's flesh, continued for two minutes.

"You stay with the car", Sergeant Mullet said to a constable.

To the other, "You come with me". They both move forward to the front entrance ready to force an entry. Vic stands behind the Sergeant ready to help when needed. A shadow moved upon the misted glass panel of the double doors, a person shuffles staggering forward, both doors burst open outward to reveal a heavily built man his head hair covered in blood which had run down his face onto his white shirt. Obviously he had been in a deadly conflict with another person and came off much worse.

"The rotten bastard"… That's all he could say in one breath and falls to his knees on the door mat, revealing a serious gash upon the crown of his head and in the left centre of his neck. Pulsating blood oozed from a severed artery, he gasps another breath and said "He's getting away … on .. out the back…I tried to stop… him… he's mad… Struck me down with the fire iron." He lost consciousness and fell to the ground in a heap.

The Lesser Evil

Jenny seeing a need leaves the car runs to assist the constable helping an injured man… She sped into the house stumbles over a body, and telephoned for an ambulance. The police enter the premises to see right through the open living space to the dining room rear bay window. A man is running across the lawn to the workshop at the back.

"That's Lesser. Stop him", said the Sergeant. Lesser started the builders truck, shunting it to effect an escape. The constable moves with leaps and bounds to his car. Vic, determined to be in at the kill, also jumps into the police car whilst it sped away along the side of the farmhouse in chase of the fleeing truck's driver.

Police Sergeant Mullet returned to see the victim with severe wounds being attended to by a constable.

"He must get into hospital soon, he's loosing too much blood, he could die within a short time."

There seems to be serious damage to a vein in his neck, the victim held back some of the blood flow with his hand pressed over the gash, whilst blood pulsated between his fingers.

"I cannot stop the bleeding; he must have urgent medical attention."

He said with the confidence of a trained nurse… Jenny returned. "An ambulance is on its way". The police car chasing after the truck along the narrow country lanes is speeding dangerously to keep the quarry in sight. Lanes, no better than muddy tracks, and often not wide enough for a small truck to travel along without brushing against the hedges either side. Vic holding onto the car's dash panel senses fear, sees fear and has fear in his nostrils. A collision is imminent. He notices the speedometer exceeding 70 miles per hour. A speed necessary to keep up with the truck yet at safe distance behind it. The police constable's driving skilfully, seeing and avoiding odd pieces of building equipment bounding about and falling out of the truck onto the narrow lanes. The truck's wheels throw out mud, grit and gravel from the puddles. The open way ahead with clear distant vision encouraged Lesser to increase speed. He's driven by a guilty conscience. The constable switches on the police siren's loud warning signals. The persistent 'He, Ha' sends the fugitive into a reckless panic, being possessed of the devil he would never yield. He's tearing through the country side and gaining speed. Suddenly a heavy agricultural tractor slides from an opening in the high hedge to enter the farm services road a short distance in front of the speeding truck, there's no avoiding a crash. Lesser instinctively stamps on the foot brake pedal, all the four wheels lock up solid, the truck accelerates over the muddy surface out of control… laughing hysterically as he sees his fate. A violent impact crash occurs as the offside centre front of the truck smashes into the tractor's heavy traction wheel. The impetus of the collision forces the agricultural machine sideways causing it to capsize, throwing the farmer clear 20 feet skidding on mud up the road. The tractor machine, absorbing the full force of the crash, is shoved into the adjacent roadside earth bank. The truck embeds itself into the underside of the tractor and everything abruptly stops dead. The sounds of cracking, tearing and wrenching fade into the distance as animals and bird life scamper in-flight from the noisy scene.

The farmer, muddied, infuriated, shaking with neurotic rage stumbles around the wreckage to reprimand the maniac truck driver. He is horror struck to see the extent of the damage done. The driver trapped by the steering column's steering wheel thrust into his face. The hub of the column shoved into his mouth and his feet trapped within the twisted cab side and floor.

"Ah."

The police constable saw the accident happen and asked the tractor driver if he as all right? He turned toward the hedge row and vomited. Vic accompanied the constable as he closely examines the accident damage and the deceased truck driver.

Vic Brandon's appalled at the sight. Lesser trapped within the wreckage. His face distorted, bruised and swollen. His eyes were ready to pop out of their sockets. The steering column had thrust his head backward with considerable force, his feet locked up within the mangled cab floor.

Whilst the constable returns to the police car to call for an ambulance and to report an incident, Vic curious about the deceased, his eyes starring horror struck looking into his Armageddon, surely something more dramatic caused that to happen? There wasn't the slightest sign of life. He must have died instantly. Studying the way the crash victim is shoved backwards and upright trapped by the steering column, Vic's eyes picked up the first clue. Thousands of small crystals and glass particles covered the cab floor and some rested upon the deceased shoulders. His curiosity drove him to look at the cab rear window opening from the outside. The shock of what he saw caused him to yell out loud,

"He's been poleaxed." He'd seen many killed in battle but this sight sickened his stomach. There had been placed in the back of the trunk a storage rack constructed of metal angled materials upon which laid many lengths of builder steel tube scaffolding poles. "It became apparent that in the collision's abrupt stop, one of the two inch diameter tubular steel poles was propelled with the same velocity as the speeding truck to be javelined through the glass rear view window to penetrate the back of Lesser's skull whilst he was thrust backward by the steering column. Only a small amount of blood was noticeable around the area where the tube had sped into the back of his head. Blood and brain may have run down inside the tube. Vic Brandon suddenly felt his own pains. He felt sick. Something like sympathy pains stabbing at his wounded forehead. His bandage had become saturated with blood, he'd lost a lot in the last two hours. Nausea swept over his whole being, he'd gone through much since yesterday and it was taking its toll. All seemed silent; there was nothing he could do. He sauntered quietly towards the police car. Every foot step jarred his head pain. He stopped to see the tractor driver sitting upon the wayside earth bank looking dismayed and distressed at the crash site. They looked at each other, there's no word to express their numbness. He continued on past to be met by the police constable leaving the car. He came directly up to Vic.

"An ambulance is on its way. It'll soon be here and Mister Hardwick with his assistant will drop in by helicopter to collect you", the constable said.

"With your wounded head it looks as if you'll need treatment fist."

Vic realised that he must be seriously injured. The binocular shattering in his face did more damage than he first thought. He considered himself lucky. The shot aimed to kill him missed its target as the wind changed and he moved his head simultaneously. The police constable, a young man, seemed to be full of enthusiasm in this particular incident.

Measuring, marking, collecting details and going about his work in a methodical way, a very efficient young man.

Vic was reclining with his face to the sunshine rather than sitting on the bonnet of the police car when he heard the chopper coming in. It hovered above the accident site acting as a marker for the ambulance arriving from the opposite direction along the country lane. It manoeuvred directly above both crash vehicles whilst John Hardwick took photographs. Jenny looked down and waved her arms intensely, overjoyed to see Vic waving back from below. He moved away from the down thrust wind from the chopper blades that partly loosened his head dressing. Half of it hung around his shoulders, he was able to grab and rebind it. The blood, thick and sticky, continued to permeate the white bandage. His face appeared pallid against the dark red congealed fluid. He cleaned his hands using the tall wet grass flourishing within the long hedge row.

Looking through the shrubbery he saw the chopper landing about 60 yards away in the same field from which the farm tractor came. He ran to enter the field eager to get into the machine. As he turned at the break in the hedgerow he ran straight into Jenny racing towards him.

She threw herself into collision with him, hugging him to let him feel her delight and relief to find he's not further hurt. She had heard the police account of the fatal accident over the radio but no mention of any other person. Her eyes sadly lifted to see his head dressing. Sighing she turned with him and together they sauntered toward the helicopter… John Hardwick had taken more photographs and as the rotor blades started spinning profusely they entered the aircraft and soon became airborne.

"I shall arrange for a police car to meet us at Dorchester, when we touch down I want you to be seen by a doctor at the hospital", said John.

"Yes of course he must." Jenny's in total agreement.

She was sitting close to him looking into his face and hugging him. His head was still hammering with pain, her closeness and reassuring smile made him feel better. He saw that she held the handcuff in her hand the other end of it still locked around her wrist. It was in his mind to ask about the handcuff and everything leading up to her abduction. There were so many questions to answer but a noisy aircraft was no place to deal with an enquiry. In the near future they will both be interviewed to give evidence and make statements then it will come out.

The police called in on the radio "EGOR! Arrangements have been made for the helicopter to land at the Dorchester football ground in the west of the town. A police car will attend to take the walking wounded to the local hospital as requested. Current matters at Veracity Farm are in the hands of Sergeant Mullet's team, they have arrested five people so far. He'll be reporting in later."

The clouds over Dorchester football ground moved eastward to leave a clear open sky. The helicopter landed close to a waiting police car in the centre of the playing field. Vic and Jenny assisted each other from the chopper to the police car. John sat in the front with the constable. Within a few minutes they were being received by a hospital doctor and a nurse with due urgency. Patients brought to hospital by the police always get prompt attention. Vic was taken immediately to the X-Ray department where it was seen that he had a wedge of glass the size of a fingernail lodged under the skin between the skull bone above the right eyebrow. This was causing the constant bleeding. More important there's a blood clot and haemorrhage from a recent heavy blow to his head, directly above his right ear. This is the cause of his head pain. He's to remain in hospital for a short while for an operation. They will drill a small hole in the skull bone which will relieve the blood clotting pressure and stop the internal bleeding. The operation is scheduled for that same evening.

John was eager to leave Dorchester. He had much to do before the end of the day and found no time for sentiments. He could do nothing further in the hospital neither could Jenny. She promised to return the following morning. She looked down hearted and sorry to leave. In saying 'Goodbye' she took both his hand in hers and he kissed each in turn. She forced a gentle smile and with an ache in her heart she left the hospital.

The Lesser Evil

NEW PERSPECTIVES

Vic Brandon awoke to a beautiful bright dawn sky. Shafts of sunlight shown through the window of the private hospital room to illuminate the wall across his bed. Fully awake he sits up, resting his back against the typical hospital iron bed head. Turning his head to the right he can see a brilliant marmalade horizontal sky. Everything out there seemed to be clean, clear, fresh and bright like a new world... He breathes deeply... filling his lungs... He wants not to miss a moment of it, he exhales slowly. The door opens the early morning tea trolley is pushed in.

"Good morning Mister Brandon, how do you like your tea?"

The nurse, no older than 19, pretty, smiling face was pouring the tea before he responded.

"Good morning nurse. Two sugars please."

She placed the drink upon the bedside locker and immediately put a clinical thermometer in his mouth. It then hit him he's a hospital patient. Lifting his hand to his forehead he felt a big soft medical dressing stuck in position by adhesive tape. A similar dressing covered a small area above his right ear. The nurse moved his hand down.

"Your head wound has been sewn up with 5 neat stitches. A piece of glass was taken away it's in the dish beside your tea cup. The other needed surgery. Your doctor will explain it to you later."

The nurse taking the thermometer out of his mouth studies it, said, "That's all right... Mister Brandon if you need to get out of bed you must

press the button hanging above you, a nurse will come to assist you."
Whatever that means?

Sipping his hot tea made him feel good, ready to face the world. He listened to the sounds from along the corridor and the wards. After the usual insipid hospital breakfast, the bed is tidied, the room is cleaned up ready for the matron's inspection preceding the doctors' rounds. Vic was advised by the doctor in his case that a glass particle removed was dangerously near his right eye. The wound will heal soon. The concussion wound is a little more serious…

"You have a small hole about 3 inches above the right ear, cutting into the skull bone at that point was a delicate and tedious operation necessary to protect the brain. I can assure you that you will fully recover. To be safe and sure I require you to remain quiet in this room for the next two days, during that time I will visit you twice daily." He didn't say who drilled the hole… "One thing you don't want: 'A hole in your head'" Vic said frivolously to himself. He smiled accepting the doctor's advice.

"Doctor you said quiet, does that mean no visitors for two days?"

"Yes and no news papers. In the afternoon you may receive visitors for 2 hours only. After two days you might be fit enough to be discharged."

Vic saw no pleasure being confined to hospital for two days. There was too much to do, so many questions to ask. He must talk to Jenny and John Hardwick urgently.

The predicament he finds himself in is not of his own making. He's been hoodwinked, cheated, manipulated, swindled, shot at, injured and hospitalised. Nobody could foresee that an advertisement in the press could bring about so much trouble. The last of his money was spent, things looked grim. He hoped to have got enough cash from the Lesser dealing but that never materialised. If he received any money for the drugs he'd have to declare it anyway, his situation seemed hopeless.

He consoles himself with the thoughts of Jenny. She is constantly on his mind. He's sure he's falling in love with her and she with him. A situation he is uncomfortable with at this time. The emotion is driving his thoughts, stirring his soul and tugging at his heart strings. He's never previously had to contend with such feelings. He's never been in love before and that means commitment, and responsibilities. How will he cope?

104

V J Tarry

Sounds coming from along the corridor indicate it's lunch time. He's ready for a well done steak and onions, he knows that's not likely for him. Oh, how he would love to be in the Commodore Hotel Restaurant with Jenny enjoying a well earned meal. Simply being with her makes everything appear better. Even a corned beef sandwich could be a shared pleasure.

When the lunch arrives it is put upon a bed tray in front of him.

"There's a telephone message note for you", says the nurse pointing to it just appearing from out of the side of the plate.

Vic's so pleased to get anything to relieve the tedium, he eagerly grabs the paper to read. It's from John Hardwick; He will be visiting about 2 o'clock to see how he's faring and bring events up to date. Jenny is helping the police sort out things at Veracity farm. She will be visiting his bedside about 4 o'clock. Vic feels better. There's so much he must do, so much to talk about, to know about. Being confined to hospital bed frustrates him… it's boring. He closes his eyes. He came back to life with a jerk. He's dozed after lunch. There must have been something in his drink. They did that in military hospitals he mused. It was the door opening suddenly that woke him, then in came John Hardwick. He's a very official person, a matter of fact type of man, always correct in everything he does. That's why he's the Chief Customs Officer. Under his commander like attitude he is a sympathetic human being with feelings, a nice fellow really.

John sat along side the bed made the usual greeting and said, "I'm sure you'd love to know that soon after we left you here yesterday the police at Poole were able to remove the hand cuff from Jenny's right wrist. She wants to tell you herself about her abduction and many other things to do with the Lesser affair. She's working with the police today and perhaps tomorrow. However, she will most likely be here with you about 4 o'clock."

John adopting a serious business like tone said, "Mister Brandon we have much to thank you for. Your co-operation in helping us and the police to break up the 'Lesser International smuggling racket'. You're aware that you were duped into bringing drugs into England. Occasionally ex-forces personnel who've served many years loose touch with civil life

105

like you, they're vulnerable and easily led into criminal activities without being aware of it. Had events not intervened your errand could have succeeded. You would have been approached again and gradually inveigled into a life of crime. We must confess that we used you. I'm sure you understood every thing we hoped you would do. With a little help and guidance you contributed to bring the Lesser gang into the hands of the police, here and in Europe."

Vic Brandon realised that he'd in many ways been foolish. It made him feel humble and defenceless. He's a lot wiser now and feels he deserves something. Perhaps they will give him a medal? After a short pause, John said, "I'll explain recent events;-"

Vic learnt that the scene of the Lesser demise was reported by the constable at the time. He also reported that Vic was a casualty with head wounds. Jenny was picked up before she had attended to Mister Booth's serious neck laceration wounds. He was taken to the local hospital in the police car. Whilst Jenny was leaving Veracity Farm in the helicopter two more police cars came in surrounding the place. An ambulance ordered to attend the crash site was also advised that the helicopter would act as a sky marker directing it along the country lanes to the accident site. John was able to get a perfect aerial view and photographed many aspects of the incident before the helicopter landed Vic in Dorchester hospital. Vic asked John if he knew what happened after they left, did the police take control? John kept in contact with the police to learn that 5 people were taken into custody suspected of working in the barn factory making illegal drug compounds intended for street market. Six teenage Asian girls were living confined in an annex building. They were each taken in to a care home for medical attention. Valerie Baker was found dead. She'd taken a cocktail of lethal drugs. Another woman was found shot dead on the living room floor. Special branch were called in to examine and secure the area for the present and future detailed analysis. John heaved a deep breath. This seemed already too much.

"I believe you and the constable were the last persons to see Lesser alive?" he asked.

"Yes, he was driving like a mad then crash, he's dead." Vic said shrugging his shoulders and cringing his face.

V J Tarry

John twisted his face feeling the impact. Heaving a deep breath he said, "Later you will be interviewed by a constable to make a statement, not only about the accident but also about everything leading up to it. Before you make any statement to anybody I must remind you that at our first meeting I caused you to sign the 'Official Secrets Act Document.' I tell you now that the national press are interested in this matter and it will not be long before they will be seeking to talk to you. If the press get to talk to you they will not let go until every detail is extracted from you. The Paparazzi will get your face on the front of the national news papers. Therefore I have arranged for you to be moved incognito to a military hospital later this evening. The hospital staff here have been advised that you must not receive visitors. Jenny of course will be excepted but she will have to identify herself. This is a security measure primarily for you own protection, also this whole smuggling business has far reaching consequences!" Vic's facial expression indicated he was about to ask the obvious questions. What had he ever done to deserve all this?

John steps in: "The girls; The call girls were occasionally used by persons in high executive business and government offices, even the county Members of Parliament is suspected... The present state of affairs will soon move into the hands of the National Security Agencies and I don't want you around when that happens."

Vic's not entirely clear in his mind about all this intrigue. Since it's for his own good he poses no questions; 'do it now find out later'. He had to ask one questions though, "As I left the farm Jenny was attending to Mister Booth's neck wound. What happened to him?"

"Jenny calling the ambulance probably saved his life. Blood covered his face, he really looked a mess. It was almost an hour before he entered hospital, by that time he had lost a lot of blood and could have died on route. I understand he has been sewn up and will live to give evidence. He's the most important witness, having worked with, and advised, Mr Lesser in all his illegal activities. Seemingly something went terribly wrong and they started fighting. Booth was struck several vicious blows with a fireside steel hooked poker. The hook bore into his neck vein tearing and severing as it was wrenched out, only a maniac would do a thing like that..."

107

The Lesser Evil

"I've been here over an hour. Jenny will come along later. I'm sure you'd rather see her. She will tell you a lot more. She's been working with the police since early this morning. We must keep up with events... While I think of it, I've asked the police in Southampton to take your car into their compound and check it over. You see Vic since you went hostile your car could have been interfered with. I saw it as my duty to arrange to have it checked by the police, you understand?"

Vic, adopting an official attitude and looking straight into Mister Hardwick's face said, "You have been arranging and directing my life from the first moment you said to me 'If we don't get Lesser we've got you!' Well Lesser's dead you've got me; you're still ordering and directing my life. Just like being in the bloody army, the only and important difference is the army paid me. So far I've got nothing but bloody trouble."

John immediately took the point.

"I'm so sorry. What with so many things happening in addition to my usual routine duties it never occurred to me to give you remuneration. In the next two days our pay office will be giving you an imprest account from which you will be able to draw cash."

"Thanks' for the cash account. When I receive the money I'll thank you better. Before you go I'd like to recap. I am to be moved this evening to a military hospital. Is that right?"

"Jenny will be along this evening. She will go with you and explain everything. I must leave it at that and be on my way" he said with a half smile upon his face. "Goodbye"

Vic's sitting upon the bedside trying to envisage a future for himself with Jenny: any close relationship with her could not thrive. He has nothing to offer and feels it. He never had a family life nor a long term friendship with anybody. He's always been a loner. Now something is drawing them close together. He hasn't the stamina to resist, even if he wanted to...

He's sipping his afternoon tea when the door slowly opened and Jenny peeped round it smiling all over her lovely face, her expressive eyes showing pleasure at seeing Vic. He saw not a trace of the sore lip she had. Healing and clever make-up present perfectly kissable lips. She knows he's eager to greet her affectionately and to hear the latest news. Every

108

time she's near him, as now, sitting upon the bed by his legs, she's urged to cuddle him. She was doing just that when in came the nurse to collect the tea things, the door closes behind her Vic pats up the pillows to make it comfortable for them both to sit up against the bed head with his right arm around her waist. Looking at his head patches she said, "John told me how they'd sewn you up and drilled a hole in your head bone, you'll be fit again in a few days." She was inclined to kiss his dressings…but never mind.

"I'm fit enough now, I understand they want to move me this evening."

"Yes, John asked me to take you in my car to the Naval Hospital at Portland. We should walk out of here like two ordinary people, after your doctor has discharged you. It'll look more natural in my car. It's to be a secret location that is why we don't go by taxi."

"Of course you know where this hospital is?"

"Yes, its all Navy with some Army personnel. I visited there a few weeks ago with John, you might like it. It's only for a couple of days." She said as if it was the most natural thing to do.

"Do you know what's going on? Why they are keeping me out of touch with everything?"

He hated being out of the action. He resented being a patient.

"I thought John told you everything? He was with you this morning" she replied with a quizzical smile. Suddenly, he changed the conversation to her.

"Jenny I must ask you about how Lesser managed to get you in his grasp, using you to barter for the drugs against me? You warned me about his dirty tricks. I was expecting something to happen but I never dreamt he'd grab you. He knew I would give him the drugs in exchange for you. It was at that moment you meant everything to me I instinctively knew that I loved you…" He said. Her eyes beamed with pleasure…

"The evening you left me, you said you would sleep that night in the car. You feared that you might be followed, when you left your flat and that you might be seized upon when attempting to enter the car full of drugs. You were right, to entertain such fear. Possibly Willy, the man who threatened you with a pistol or somebody else waited all night but you didn't appear", she said.

"Now an interesting question, 'who would know that you and I are in courtship together?' Certainly not Reggie Lesser. Only one name comes to mind, Simon Sinclair. I rejected his advances many times and he has seen us at least twice at The Commodore. The last time I snubbed him and he spoke to you and departed. That's by the way... The morning of my abduction as I left my residence to walk around to my car a taxi pulls up alongside me. The driver asked, "You Jenny?"

"Yes"

"Vic Brandon wants me to take you to him. He's in an office at Winton. I'm to tell you it's urgent." He said in a matter of fact sort of way.

"Why what's the matter is he hurt?"

"I only know that he phoned to instruct me to collect you that's all."

"It occurred to me that something had gone wrong with the plan, I'm worried. As soon as I enter the cab we drove speedily through traffic, during the journey the cab driver uttered no word. I could only think that you were taking refuge somewhere perhaps from an attack or siege. The cab drove into a yard with lorries, trailers and containers it stopped at the entrance to an office cabin arrangement. The cab driver said that he thought that this was the place he had to bring me. He helped me out of the cab, escorted me to the door and opened it. Everything's quiet. Unusually still, more like a Sunday. Looking around I saw a haulage vehicle operators premises. One might expect to find somebody about the place, there wasn't anybody. The yard was muddy after recent rain churned up by lorries movements and a distinct smell of diesel fuel in the air, lorry wheels, old tyres and things laying against the outer tin clad fencing. This is the sort of place where Tony would have kept his lorry and trailer when not in use", she said and stopped talking. Vic's not comfortable, he has pins and needles sensation in his fingers

Jenny moves herself from the bed, sitting beside it again she continues:- "I turned to face the Porter Cabin come office entrance door. The cab drives away. I felt desperately alone. Vic's here somewhere, he urgently needs me, I must find him. I called out loudly 'Vic Brandon it's Jenny here, where are you?' A muffled voice said come inside... down

110

the passage to the right. Thinking only that you needed me I went into a small office room. Looking around there was nobody to be seen. A sound behind me I turned to see the door shutting. I grabbed the handle a moment too late, it snapped secure locking me inside. I panicked, tried to pull it open but to no avail. I was trapped like a rat in a cage. Feverishly I started looking for anything that could be used to aid an escape from this prison. I ransacked the office desk throwing out papers and pornographic magazines. The telephone: call for help, reaching out across the desk, I was just about to grab the handset. It gave me a jerk like an electric shock. It started ringing the moment I touch it. Hesitantly... Wondering who? I lift the receiver, with an instinctive reaction. I snapped out an angry ' Hello'.

A smarmy voice spoke so placidly "Hello Jenny, It's Reggie Baker here". I'd not heard from him for more than two years. "I'm so sorry to have brought you into this situation. Now listen, I need your help", he said. "It's important, now listen."

I might have guessed that he was behind my abduction. I suppressed my seething anger to learn what he would want me to do.

'Are you listening?' I was trembling with rage, the swine's trapped me and wants my help.

"Yes" I replied with bitterness in my heart and my voice.

"I'm sure you are aware that I am to meet your Vic Bwandon this morning in a field near Wareham. He's got something I want." Before he could finish I burst out that I know a car load of filthy drugs.

"You know, I don't need to explain the situation... I've got something he wants: you Jenny. Your affectionate admirer would willingly swap you for my car, don't you think? I'm sure he would."

"You want me as a bargaining factor, that's a lousy rollen trick further it's despicable." I groaned over phone at him.

"Exactly Jenny you're quick on the uptake. When you and I meet Vic Bwandon the deal will be simple. I shall hand you over in exchange for my car. Whilst you two are consoling each other I'll drive away that will end the matter. My main concern is getting my car back. I shall not hurt you" He said in a smarmy conceited voice. I hated the man."

"Vic I then recalled previous discussions. It was necessary to get the car full of drugs into Lesser's possession. He seems to be playing into our hands and I wasn't going to do anything to deter him. I wasn't going to make it too easy either...

'You have me trapped in this office against my will. That's kidnapping and I shall have a few words about that when I see you' and I meant it.

'Jenny I know I have walked all over your pride and esteem, for that I apologize but please don't compound the issue. I need you only as trading commodity, it will put you into the arms of the man you want

'How would you know a thing like that. How'd you know what I want?'

'Never mind. I am well informed' he said. 'Now listen carefully. If you co-operate fully there'll be no trouble'

'No trouble? How shall I know you will keep your word. You've lied, swindled and cheated Vic Brandon, that's how we've got into this filthy drugged mess. No I don't trust you...' It hurt and angered my mind that he was indirectly responsible for Tony's death and arranged a faked accident. He's too smarmy. I felt more repulsed with every word he spoke."

'I am however your prisoner and I will only co-operate so long as it serves my purpose to do so' She knew these were only brave words. She's mindful not to say or do anything to jeopardise their plan and put Vic in peril. 'OK then you'll go along with me... You won't regret it.' She shrugs her shoulders in contempt.

'I'll be along to pick you up in about 20 minutes time. You will find sufficient facilities to make yourself a coffee whilst you're waiting. I should remind you that you are using the only phone in the office, it, is a direct line to me. There's no outside line." He said and hung up...

Vic could see in Jenny's eyes and the expression on her face that she was annoyed, deeply hurt. The incident she related humiliated her. For a few moments they were quiet... "Before he released me from my captivity, he handcuffed me to his waist belt. He's only interest is getting me to the bargaining field. He drove the open Land rover like a possessed maniac. I felt great fear in my heart like driving toward a precipice" Vic stopped her on that. He was able to figure the rest of her captivity and subsequent bartering presentation in the field. He rightly supposed that

112

the bag over her head was a shock tactic, gagging to prevent her shouting a warning.

Jenny's eyes stared in horror into Vic's she asked: "He's dead isn't he? You saw the way he died didn't you?"

Her body shivered with cold fear as she spoke. Vic takes her hand into his to steady her, support and comfort her. She was not consoled by Vic's words she had a premonition that something was wrong. In trepidation she said.

"You must tell me. I must know from you as a first hand witness. Lesser is dead and his evil is dead with him, isn't it?" she pleaded.

"Jenny I can assure you that he's dead. Nobody could have survived the disaster that hit him. He's completely finished, he couldn't be more dead."

She heaved a deep breath. Her bosom rose as her chest expanded. She was free of the foreboding that had hung over her ever since she learnt of Tony's death. She wanted vengeance, she hated everything she'd found out about Lesser. Heeding Vic's words she's relieved of the pain and hatred of vengeance. She became silent, placid for a minute...

It showed on her face that she wanted to say something. Vic looked straight at her.

"Well come out with it then. What's worrying you now?", he asked.

She hesitated... "Something personal I think you should know."

Jenny closed her eyes as if to recall passed events, her eyes remained closed a moment longer as she spoke.

"When the police woman constable came to tell me that Tony my husband was killed in an accident. I somehow knew it was true, although I had spoken to Tony late upon the previous day in the evening. Something swept over me as he spoke. I felt there was something seriously wrong in the abrupt way his words sounded." She paused then opened her eyes.

"The news of his death stabbed directly into my hart, body and soul because I was in an advanced state of pregnancy and totally alone. I had nobody to whom I could turn, no shoulder to cry on. I felt hopelessly deserted. I shut myself away from the world and cried and cried. I had to get it out of my soul, ridding myself of my grief took many days. Being a young widow was not for me, it's ridiculous and painful. I had to come to terms with it…As you know I contacted the Customs Office at Poole and met John Hardwick. He was helpful, sympathetic and perhaps he saw that I could be useful to the H.M Customs and be particularly useful to his office. He offered me a job; 'Clerical Assistant'. I needed that job to bring me to life again and I had to have an income. I wasn't inclined to go back to the tourist business in my condition, I took the job not intending to make a career out of it. About 5 weeks later I was required to attend an inquiry into Tony's fatal accident in Livorno, Italy. John Hardwick had shown considerable interest in my case. He arranged for me to travel with him to Italy expenses paid. We made a friend of a local Newspaper reporter. Together we gathered a lot of vital information about how and why Tony died. All the time in Italy I felt something stifling me, particularly when I saw the place where his lorry crashed into the ravine. Tragic, nausea hit me in the stomach and it wrenched my mind. The next day about lunch time I felt very ill. We left on the afternoon flight. During the flight I was feeling pains in my lower abdomen. Immediately the plane landed at Gatwick an ambulance rushed me to hospital; my baby miscarried, the pregnancy aborted. This ordeal left me physically and mentally exhausted and stranded with only what I stood up in. I couldn't help myself I cried most of the time. Monday morning I was discharged from the hospital feeling very weak. I could hardly stand. I was met by a taxi to take me to my home in Poole, arrange by John Hardwick. A note said simply 'Take the week off you'll feel better'. I began to feel much better after a few days but my body and mind had suffered more than I realised. I had to recover my health and figure and regulate my mind. A week later I signed up with a fitness training course. I still attend every Friday afternoon it's so good for me.

"That was nearly two years ago", she said with some relief in her voice. Vic saw that she suffered tension whilst telling him about her miscarriage and consequential pain to her body and mind. No man can fully feel or understand what a woman goes through in child birth. How could he? He's made different but by feeling as best he could with her, it grieved him sorely. He'd suffered, seen and known suffering.

"Thanks Jenny, thanks for telling me all about that, it helps to forge a bond of understanding between us", he smiled, her face changed she knew he felt for her. She moved forward to kiss him, in so doing laid her-

114

self more by accident than intent uniformly upon him. The effect of this caused his stomach to flutter and the blood to surge excitedly through his veins, a prelude of future pleasures. She knew she'd pleased him and brought similar pleasure to herself. They heard movement in the corridor outside. She sped to sit upon the chair close by his bed as the room door opened to admit his Doctor. The Doctor saw his patient's face flushed. Usually Doctor's take their patient's pulse. In this case he just looked at his charge.. Had he felt Vic's pulse he might have been alarmed, it was rising with excitement…

"Mister Brandon, I understand you wish to be discharged to another hospital this evening?"

"Yes", he said looking at Jenny "and she will be taking me in her car if that's alright with you Doctor?" He nodded approval.

"You will be able to collect your clinical notes from the nurse before you leave. Take it a little easy from now on." Did he suspect something.

Vic's clothing had been put through the laundry. Blood stains and mud removed and nothing pressed. His trouser hung from his waist like old sacking. They laughed as he stepped into the only suit he possessed.

"It feels clean and I'm rid of the blemishes of the last few days."

Jenny offered her vanity mirror. He looked dishevelled with facial stubble having not shaven since the night before he slept in the car. Some hair had been cut off over his right ear, giving an unbalance hair style and two patches stuck to his head.

"I look a mess don't I?" He said in a subdued voice.

"Underneath you're a courageously handsome man. I want you to know it." She said with apparent pride. She flung her arms vigoursly around him, hugging and holding him. As if taking ownership of a coveted treasure, her man. Together they walked like two ordinary people out into the cool sobering evening air. Two other people passed them going in toward the Reception desk. They noticed both men carried cases of equipment often used by press reporters. Their steps quickened toward Jenny's parked car, eager to get away unnoticed.

"You're an unusually good driver. Women have not enjoyed a good reputation for driving." He gave her a compliment she nodded in recognition.

The Lesser Evil

"You know my car is in the police compound since yesterday. I am not told which compound or when I may get it back. Do you know anything about it?", he asked her.

"No! It's the first I've heard of it. I'm sure John will know, but why did the police take your car?"

"They supposed that it could have been booby trapped whilst standing overnight in the Southampton Car park", he said. "John asked the police to check it out."

"That's an awful thing to do, booby trapping. I could believe that evil man Lesser being capable of such an atrocity. It's sensible of John to have your car checked, I'd hate to…", she stopped herself. She could not think of Vic in an explosion.

He immediately asked; "Jenny, could you find time to call in at my flat tomorrow to collect my toiletries and a few items of clothing for me?"

"Vic, that's the least I can do of course you'll give me the key later. Would you like me to bring anything else?"

"No. You're a darling. I'd be happy just to see you. I have a feeling I'll be very lonely in the hospital without you."

The car drives into the Naval base. The male nurse receives them in the entrance to the very military looking hospital. Everything appeared to have been very recently painted and decorated. All ship-shape and Bristol fashion. The room into which Vic is to bedded separates from the main Wards and is furthest from the entrance.

"No visitors after 21:00 hours", the nurse said and reels off a few standing orders which must be adhered to daily.

Vic looked downhearted, but before he could make any comment Jenny said, "It's only for two days, you'll soon be back with us again. Come walk with me back to the car."

Vic would have walked with her to the end of the earth. This time it's good night and parting until tomorrow. He opened the car door quickly. Jenny stood back sharply he took her in his arms turned her upon her heel and kissed her… A lingering longing kiss. In that kiss Jenny could feel his despair and loneliness. She hugged him the feelings mutual. Without prolonging the agony she slowly turned, entered the car and drove away. He sauntered back to the room, his thoughts with her. Vic reclines upon
116

the bed, his head supported in the palms of his folded hands behind his neck. Looking around the place he can't help feeling he's missing the action outside. The urge to be in 'the thick of it' only drove his mind... He sees 'The National Security Agents' searching and finding information, implicating people; examining every part of the farm house premises, collecting evidence of illegal and criminal activities. Interviewing, questioning people and getting statement; tedious long drawn out; every word measured; statements. Vic's envious of those out there not confined to hospital. He realises if he were available he might be in a police station giving statement about Mister Bakers fatal accident and the car load of drugs he brought into the country. It's affected him the events of the past days. It's change him in so many ways. He'll live a meaningful life, be a model citizen, making everything count – from meeting people and making friends. He's sure the whole experience worked to strengthen his self-esteem, his dignity, and attitude toward his future. Citizen Brandon.

He's taking responsibility for himself, realizing people cared and thought about him, especially Jenny; she's wonderful...

Vic wakes to a familiar routine common within most military establishments. Although he is separated in a room on his own, nothing has changed even the breakfast foods the same, eaten in the mess hall. His room, simple, uninteresting like a prison cell. He hates it, he must get out. There's a confusion of voices outside. He listens intently trying to catch a few words. Two men enter the room; "I'm Commander Bennet, the hospital physician." If he hadn't said such it wouldn't be apparent. He carried no insignias of rank or authority; he spoke kindly and politely. Turning curiously to the other man behind him, said to Vic Brandon, "I understand this gentleman wishes you to sign a receipt for money due to you."

The physician steps aside to read his patient's notes. The other man moves forward, obviously feeling his intrusion, thanked the Doctor.

"Mister Vic Brandon," the man explained he was from the Admiralty pay office. He gave Vic ready cash and a postal order for more. The total might be a months pay. Now things are looking up. Vic signed for the cash and the order. The cashier left as quickly as he came, "Goodbye gentlemen."

The Lesser Evil

The Surgeon Commander came to his patient. Spoke in a friendly manner, whilst looking intently into his eyes, noting that everything seemed to be in order. Vic aware of the curiosity in the doctor's face asked, "Doctor, do you know John Hardwick, he arranged for me to be here?"

"Yes, we are old friends and good comrades. He spoke to me about your case yesterday. You may stay here as long as it serves your purpose. But for now you're a patient in my care. I wish to see both your head wounds." He commences to remove the simple dressings.

"The stitches could come out tomorrow. The operation is hardly visible only a small scar... you're healing well. How are you feeling? Any more headaches?"

"Thank you Doctor everything is back to normal."

"That's fine. I'll have the nurse put new dressing upon your wounds soon." The doctor moves to the door and stops a moment, "I understand John Hardwick is visiting you here later today." He said as he was leaving.

A nurse arrived with naval precision re-dressed his wounds and left.

He's determined to get out of this confinement and will tell John in no uncertain terms: 'I'm a civilian get me out of here'.

Midmorning coffee available in the wardroom saw him sitting alone feeling shabby reading the daily newspapers. He's surprised to find so little about Lesser's fatal demise. 'Lorry's fatal collision with tractor', the article purports to explain in few words only what happened. Nothing mentioned about the cause of the accident or identity of the deceased. No reference to witnesses or police. The whole incident had been made to appear unimportant; insignificant, just another accident.

Vic knows that John Hardwick is the only man with sufficient influence to restrict the press in this way: perhaps by offering a more sensational story later, he believes its being done for his own good and that all will be explained in due course.

He feels a state of frustration eating into his soul. He can walk out of the hospital any time he wishes. He knows it would be deserting the only two people who care about him, the only friends he has.

V J Tarry

Vic Brandon stood up, eager to receive John Hardwick's' hand in greeting. Looking into John's face he could see that he had something important to tell him. They both sit, John upon the only chair in the bedroom.

"There's a lot I have to tell you", he said looking sullen.

"I spoke to Jenny about an hour ago, she will be visiting you here about 4 o'clock. She told me you asked her to get things from your flat. She was unable to get anything. It appears that during the night or early morning when you slept in the car somebody kicked the door down and lobbed in an incendiary device. Although the fire was contained within your flat everything was destroyed."

Vic jerked upright shocked at the news.

"Everything's' gone, all my worldly goods, all my papers, passport, birth certificate, my life's history wiped out. Is that what's happened, I'm destitute, ruined. I have only what I stand up in."

"I'm sorry that I had to tell you this. You should also know the police have closed your flat for forensic investigation. They will be seeking to talk to you about it later. I'm sure you'll have no difficulty in naming the person behind this criminal act, but I don't want you to give the police any names." John looked to get Vic's reaction to his words.

"Everything's gone, just like that. I've been wiped out"… He heaves a deep breath to relieve the immediate tension and choking in his throat; his body seized in anguish. He felt physically sick. He places the palm of his right hand upon his forehead and feels again the pains and frustrations he endured. He must be mad to tolerate all this trouble.

"It's all for nothing. I'm a great big idiot getting involved with your stunt to entice Lesser into your trap. You Customs people got what you wanted and I'm your virtual prisoner in this hospital with nothing but pains and disappointment for helping you. I feel so stupid. I'm so bloody annoyed I could easily use four letter words to express my anger…If I had any common sense left in my body I'd walk out of this bloody mess."

The Lesser Evil

It then stabbed his mind. He has no place to go, no car, no friends outside. His instilled sense of duty directed his thoughts. He stopped himself; put his face in his hands to shut out the world… He realized that the only way out of this tragic situation is to go forward. He remembered that he agreed to co-operate in the outset even devised his own plan to get Lesser entrapped to avenge the hurt caused to Jenny and in some way hopefully compensate himself.

He lifted his head to see John sitting, patiently staring at him waiting for a response. Vic grinned, then laughed at his own predicament.

"Well, have you got any other drastic news to cheer me up?" he said with sarcasm in his voice.

"I understand your feelings; your hurt. I would like you to know that I will make sure that you will be fully compensated for your assistance and losses incurred whilst helping me and my department.

Vic's spirits rose a little at the words "fully compensated". Whatever that means. He'll have to wait for that to materialize.

"John! I'll have to leave this hospital soon, but I have no place to go now. I must get another flat somewhere and that could take a couple of weeks perhaps longer."

"Yes of course. I'll be able to get you into the 'Strand Hotel' it's on beach road. It overlooks the sea to the east. You passed it coming here. The manager, James Gordon, is a friend and business acquaintance. I'm sure he will accommodate you in style. The hotel has a first class restaurant with weekend dance floor entertainment during the season. You may remain there week after each week accountable. You will pay only for your meals and drinks. I'll arrange everything for you"

"Thanks, I'll be eager to get the stitches out and get into the hotel. Will it be sufficient for me to report to the reception desk, will somebody be informed? Will there be a booking in my name?" Vic's ego rose a little.

"Relax, you're too excited. Yes, all care will be taken to fit you in. Report to the desk about midday tomorrow. I'll ask Jenny to help you move. I must now remind you again that you are bound by the 'Official Secrets Act'. Whilst you're in the hotel, you must be careful not to talk about anything that happened to any of us, since you brought the car

120

load of illegal drugs into this country." John emphasised the words 'illegal drugs'. He mentions the national press. Headlines, 'Racketeering and drug trafficking' Reggie Lesser used every trick known to the legal and criminal profession. Lesser's friend and life long associate, Brian Booth, a Barrister at Law is under arrest in hospital. "Vic you must be careful what you say to people." Vic nodded his understanding.

"I told you this whole affair is in the hands of the Special Branch. It's exploded since then to involve ministers in Government both here and abroad. Many incriminating documents were seized. Huge amounts of money in various foreign currencies taken from the farm house. 'Interpol' entered the hotel Vigliana in Italy taking documents and two men into custody, then they sealed up the place. The same day Italian police working with Interpol entered the factory building of the International Freight Forwarding Organisation in Livorno taking possession of documents, money and pertinent materials. Many arrests have been made, many others have fled the scene. The amount of drugs seized here and abroad have not yet been assessed but it's considered to be a vast quantity in various forms, shapes and sizes mostly in the distribution chain of supply extending across the country and into most of Europe. The Special Branch working with Scotland Yard are studying every detail of the finds at the Veracity Farm. A great assortment of evidence has been collected and is now being documented." Observing the enthusiasm in Vic's face John continues, "one particular item of interest is a tape recording equipment used to log every incoming call with many taped message reels were taken. The recorded messages were from a private line...when Jenny and I were in Livorno remember Mark was able to get two telephone numbers calls from the hotel Vigliana to England. One such number Jenny claimed as hers. The other I enquired about. The Genaral Post Office GPO said that number is a public call box at the east end of the Village Rigby in north Dorset. Looking at the ordinance survey map Vilage Rigby the callbox is about 1 mile from Veracity farm house. The actual telephone box is in a position on the corner of a lane with the road against a hedge. The other side of that hedge is a meadow, part of Veracity Farm", he said.

Before John continued Vic interjects the question, "Why would anybody telephone a public callbox in Dorset from a hotel in Italy?"

The Lesser Evil

If I remember correctly it was late at night when the call was made. Could anybody be expected to be waiting for such a haphazard call?"

John responds immediately to Vic's questions.

"No, nobody was required to wait. The callbox had a secretly tapped telephone line to the farm house. The GPO had no knowledge of it. When calls come into this call box line it rings six times. If then not answered a cleverly hidden outside device automatically switches the call to a tape recorder in the farm house. Presumably to avoid any general post office record being made of such private secret calls. However, I'm sure we will learn a lot more when the tapes have been studied", said John, and made ready to leave

Vic responded, "It must be that only a few of Lesser's gang would know about that call box."

"Yes I'm sure your right… good bye"

Vic stood patiently at the hospital entrance looking at the late afternoon summer sky; feeling the pleasant effect of the sun's warmth on his face. He's eagerly waiting Jenny's arrival. She's a few minutes late when her car drives by whilst he has his head in the clouds. She hastily walks from the car park carrying a weekend bag to be greeted with a kiss on her cheek. Vic took the bag into the building and opened it in the room. She'd brought everything a man could need and a jazzy pyjama. She must have stretched her imagination to get everything just right.

"It's so thoughtful of you to bring all this toiletry and apparel. I've so far had to cope with what I could scrounge."

He took her in his arms, she smiling at her achievement knowing she'd pleased him, yielding to his embrace they kissed affectionately. He'd never known anybody caring for his needs and wellbeing. The thought lifts his ego and entered his heart, he drew her closer and again kissed her.

It was a kiss that went through them and flowed gracefully about them. They were at that moment unconscious of everything except each other…

"Jenny it's lovely to see you. Sit upon the bed beside me I'd love to talk to you. You know John was with me earlier and told me about my flat being destroyed by fire. Were you able to enter to see the damage?"

122

V J Tarry

"No, not entirely. A police constable was guarding the entrance pending a fire officer's inspection. From what I saw everything was burnt beyond redemption... I realized that I'd have to buy everything you needed and John told me to charge it to my expense account."

He then saw she grieved for his loss; her sorrow spoke more than words.

"It hit hard when John told me about the fire. I've lost everything. It's as if by some quirk of fate my past life has been wiped out I'll have to start all over again."

"Vic. I've been thinking about starting life again. Living alone is not for me. It's often boring. Since I've met you I'm sure we could make a wonderful life together. From the first time I saw you in the German Court; I think I knew. I attended that court with some vengeance in mind. I expected to see a gangster; the type who might have killed my husband. I saw you. I observed you; you the man who came to claim the car load of drugs and drive it back to England. I was required to be able to identify you later in case of a prosecution. Previously I was not given your advertisement in the newspaper. I was given very little information about the man I was to observe before going to Court. I was sitting in the front row when you arrived. I carefully noted everything about you. The way you moved, your military bearing, the efficient way you addressed the Court. I could not see you as a drug smuggler; you just did not seem to be the type. I began to see you as a handsome, perhaps naive, errant Knight. I was standing close behind you whilst you thanked the bench for the papers you received. Suddenly you turned, stepping backwards you collided with me. For a few magical moments our eyes met in harmony, I observed sincerity in your face, then for a moment my heart flipped. I experienced a flash of wisdom a sort of premonition that our destinies would link... I'm sure you knew it" she said.

"Although I didn't realise it at that moment, something unusual hit me. It must have been your demure charms, your personality and polite way you spoke only a few words. Yes I knew it then and know it now. I'm sure we are meant for each other. We'll make a lovely pair together."

In her he saw a new future, a new life separate from anything he'd ever known.

The Lesser Evil

"As soon as I'm able to get things sorted out I'd love us to set up house and home together. I must first get suitable gainful employment and settle down."

Jenny knew what he felt, she wanted the same. They talked in detail about their future and agreed to be secretly engaged... He stood looking at his lady love amazed at what he'd done. For the first time in his life he's become engaged and to an attractive accomplished woman. Furthermore he said to Jenny those simple effective words:- "I love you" those words seemed inadequate.

He then shouted the word to the world to hear, "I love you, Jenny I love you." He's filled with self righteousness and conceit, he's in love for the very first time, it's wonderful.

He holds Jenny closely to his heart and said:- "I love you. I've never said those words to any woman before. That makes it so much more meaningful for me, for you, for us."

Suddenly Vic burst into laughter, looking at Jenny, "What a place to get engaged; a private room in a Naval hospital; it's romantic, rather funny. You read about incidents like this in magazines."

Excitement prompted his urge to lay her across the bed, her eyes fixed on his as she saw his intent... The door burst open and in rushed a male nurse, "I heard you yell out are you alright?"

———

Saturday morning Vic's discharged from the hospital after the withdrawal of stitches, both wounds are patched up. Jenny returns to collect his few things and together they drove to the Strand Hotel. A double room on the fourth floor with views across the road and the beach to the open sea had been reserved for him.

"This is much better, more to my liking. Here we will find ourselves and happiness." He joyously said to Jenny.

Jenny turned from the window full of self satisfaction and happily moved to Vic and gently put her arms around his neck pressing her lithe body firmly against his. She felt that it aroused him; it was a way of showing her appreciation. Everything pleased her, she anticipates a joyous weekend with her fiancé. Later they were leaving the hotel together. He stopped, staring at a displayed notice. There was to be a Balalaika band entertainment that evening after dinner. They found the only available table for two in an alcove across the dance floor. It couldn't have been better. He immediately booked it.

They walked the short distance to the shopping centre purchasing a suit and other clothing for him. Vic loved dressing up smartly and received good advice and a dinner jacket made especially for that evening. Jenny bought only a few personal things. She had not decided what she would wear that evening, wishing to keep her attire a secret until appearing in the restaurant for dinner. In her career she'd developed a sense of occasion and loved to surprise people.

After their lunch she drove away to prepare herself for the evening. Explaining that she needed all the time to do her hair and arrange everything and that she would arrive at the hotel by taxi about 7.30pm.

Vic had much to do reconnoitring his new location and laying out clothing for the evening. Never before had he ever dressed in civil attire for dinner. He's decided to make this occasion successful and memorable. Checking every detail, the weather is set fine for the weekend with night time temperatures around 72 degrees. He phones the desk asking if it would be possible to get a dozen red roses to be displayed upon their table in the alcove. They will do what they can and let him know.

He's pleased to find all the usual bathroom shower gels, cosmetics etc etc. Grooming himself boosted his ego, being scrubbed up beautifully, he's determined to be worthy of Jenny's love. Her words echo in his head, "You're a courageously, handsome man and I want you to know it."

He heaves a deep breath, expanded his chest and stood tall. Vic's feeling great, he's enthusiastic about their weekend together. The bedside phone rings. The desk informed him the roses he ordered will be placed upon their table shortly and that dinner will be served at 7.30.

"Thank you. Just one more thing. I've always had difficulty tying my bow tie, will you please send somebody to help me?"

Within a few minutes the headwaiter arrived. "Twelve, beautiful red roses have been placed on your table in a suitable cut glass vase, it's a magnificent display. May I ask Sir for what purpose?" Vic looks directly

125

at the correctly dressed man standing in front of him and proudly said, "Yesterday I became engaged to a lovely lady. She does not know it yet although I think she's guessed it that we will celebrate the occasion this evening."

These are the words headwaiters like to hear, they love to make the event go smoothly and efficiently.

"Congratulations, Sir. I'll have the pleasure of meeting the lady when I seat you both at your table. About the rose display sir, may I suggest twelve roses will impair your ability to see your fiancé across a table for two? One rose would be more effective and meaningful, the rest we could place upon the coffee table here in your room."

"Thank you. That's good thinking. I want everything to be perfect this evening."

"You requested help with your tie Sir. This being a special evening might I be allowed to attend to your complete dress, turning you out immaculately?"

"Why, Yes of course, anything", Vic said with great pleasure at the suggestion, he'd never had a valet dressing him previously.

He's loving this attention, realizing that he's not only a man but also a gentleman. He's standing in front of a full length mirror, his valet attending to every detail: setting his tie right, forming his hair, trimming his moustache, fitting and adjusting his dress. The waiter is pleased with his work and his man.

"Sir, your military bearing enhances your complete attire, you carry yourself well. I'm sure you'll both enjoy your dinner, dance and the floor entertainment. It's a full house, every table booked." The waiter said.

"Thank you." "Oh, before you leave will you please have a bottle of champagne placed upon the table with the rose?"

"Yes sir"

Vic stands upon the top step of the hotel entrance looking out across to the summer evening sky… Guests are taking their seats in the restaurant. It's past 7.30, Vic's getting anxious there's no sign of a taxi with Jenny…

He looks at his watch it's 7.45. He lifts his eyes to see a taxi across the road turning a half circle to sweep around, to stop right outside the hotel
126

where Vic's standing. He steps forward to help Jenny enter the hotel where upon she quickly slips into the foyer whilst Vic attends to the cab fare.

Everybody is seated, the foyer is deserted when Jenny reappears. She moved graciously to stand under the chandelier. Spears of golden light reflect from her golden bronze hair and dazzle him. He just stood bewildered gazing at her radiance... Her beautifully simple white evening dress embraced her figure in ancient Grecian style. She's ravishingly lovely as if she had just stepped out of a Hollywood film, a Grecian Goddess

"Vic", she could see his eye fixed on her, "Shall we move forward to the restaurant?"

She takes his arm. He's proud of her, he must make their entrance classically dignified. They enter to be met by the head waiter who's momentarily surprised by her loveliness. The waiter leads on to escort them across the floor to their table. The pair move slowly and gracefully. Voices stop and heads turn toward them: 'They could be celebrities'.

Seated they order from the menu and of course champagne to enhance the occasion. Vic cannot take his eye off her. She has gone to such lengths to make herself attractive for him. He lifts his glass to her, she smiles, taking her glass to her lips, she hesitates, her eyes shine and dance a little, "To our future happy life together", she said.

"I'll drink to that and to the magic that brought us together," he said.

They stared at each other lovingly and, as the waiter filled their glasses again, Vic reached over the red rose and kissed her luscious lips with a passion he'd been saving for that moment...

They were enjoying the last of their five course dinner when Vic noticed a well built distinguished looking tall gentleman with a smartly trimmed beard, dressed in a white suit approaching their table. He spoke to them politely excusing his approach. He said, "I'm James Gordon the manager of the hotel. I am pleased to receive you both as my guest."

Vic stands up to take James's hand, "I'm Vic Brandon and this lady is Jenny Robin..." he stopped there.

James said, "John Hardwick told me about how you'd helped him, also he mentioned that Jenny might appear. That's why you have a table for two in the alcove. We wish to make your stay comfortable. By the way please use my first name, James."

The Lesser Evil

He's looking intently at Jenny. He reaches out offers his hand she stand to receive his gesture. "I'm delighted to receive such a charming lady guest, please enjoy yourselves." He smiled, enhancing his personality.

"John Hardwick never mentioned that I would meet such a delightfully charming lady... My head waiter tells me that you two love birds became engaged yesterday."

Jenny coyly nods her head whilst turning toward Vic who smiles and nods acknowledgement. James congratulates them both and told the waiter to put a bottle of champagne on their table, compliments of the house.

"We are being entertained by a seven piece Balalaika band this evening. Would you mind if I announce your engagement? That sort of thing always makes everything go along comfortably, customers love romantic occasions?"

They both respond to James.

"Yes, why not tell the world we are in love, it will make this moment more memorable."

The drums tremble, roll and stop to attract the guests attention...

"Ladies and Gentleman I have great pleasure tonight to announce the engagement of Miss Jenny Robin and Mister Vic Brandon. They are both with us here to celebrate their engagement and good fortune."

James turns to the couple, lifting his left arm toward the alcove, "Ladies and Gentleman please raise your glasses... I give you our honoured engaged couple Jenny and Vic."

The dinner guests made the usual responses with their glasses. A few came to congratulate them personally. The band master came to ask their choice of music to which they were required to lead the dance. Lovers often like to associate a popular song or a tune to bring back memories of a particular loving occasion. They looked to each other for an answer:- Jenny catching the spirit of the dance, looking passionately into Vic's eye, simply said: "I'll be loving you always".

"That's our song, it's a nice slow waltz, it'll be very fitting." Vic said to the band leader. The Balalaika band had many stringed instruments soft and suitable for Waltzes and love songs. Yes, they could play it.

128

James steps back and announces from the floor, "Our most charming newly engaged couple have chosen a waltz to open the dance floor, Ladies and Gentlemen, please take your partners for the ever popular slow waltz, I'll be loving you always."

The lights dimmed making the mood soft and romantic, Jenny moves into Vic's arms and feels secure. She snuggles into him with her head upon his shoulder. They make a handsome pair...He held her so tight it took her breath away. She lifted her head, there was no doubt in her mind that she loved him. Her hair brushed his cheek and they kissed, a passionate kiss that put the seal upon their engagement.

"Congratulations to both of you. If I'd known that you were getting engaged I would have brought you both a present." They both turn to the speaker, surprised to see John Hardwick dancing with his wife along side of them.

"I suspected that you two were doing things, now we know. Would you like to join us at our table by the big window after the dance? I'd like you to meet Dawn my wife."

The 'love birds' danced the same waltz again. Somebody asked for it in their honour, many loved the popular old tune, in particular the effective tremolo way it was played made it sound mysteriously different. They were happy to dance it again, the words began to get into their hearts and minds. She was touched by the gesture, her heart seemed to lurch and fly to her feet, she could have danced all night.

The Lesser Evil

DAWN'S RING

The champagne they drank had its intended effect. They both felt in a happy mood and ready to meet Dawn. John stood to welcome them to their table. He formally introduced Jenny and Vic to Dawn Hardwick...

"Aw shut up with your official attitude, these beautiful young people are here to enjoy themselves, they don't want formalities... save it for your office."

Dawn was a charming lady with character. She knew how to deal with formalities. John in his naval career had to preside over many official and ceremonial functions to which she attended, but she wasn't having any of it here... She takes Jenny's hand holding it affectionately. Her eyes studied Jenny face, she pulls her hand closer to hold it near to her heart.

"My dear, you're a charming lady. I can see you have character and good dress sense. If I had a daughter I'd like her to be just like you." She'd taken to her straight away. "My dear, may I see your engagement ring."

"I'm sorry, NO. We hadn't time to get one. We only got engaged yesterday when Vic was a patient in hospital. We did not think that tonight would turn into our engagement party. We made no preparation, sent out no invitation. It was only James Gordon's announcement that started it up here", Jenny said.

V J Tarry

"How extraordinary and so romantic for you. These official things are done in the best society but I would have preferred an elopements so much more exciting, much more romantic don't you think?"

The dear lady Dawn studies Jenny's hand takes a ring from her own finger and spontaneously slips it onto Jenny's finger.

"There, it fits perfectly as if it was made for you." Jenny wasn't ready to receive such a gift but before she could politely reject it Dawn said, "Now don't give me any nonsense about you can't accept it. It's perfect for you, for this moment and for your engagement."

She reaches out to Vic's hand pulling him into the scene. He sees the lady take the ring again into her own hand and pass it over to him. Vic's surprised.

"You have an engagement ring now you put it on your fiancé's finger, say a few endearing words to her. It will delight my heart to see her receive it and to know you're in love."

She looked at them both, turned to face John and said, "We were lovers just like you two".

John replied, "Lovers we still are although the passion and fire has died down we still love each other, we have been together over 30 years."

Dawn nodding in agreement, "I was 19 years old. John a handsome Naval officer just swept me off my feet. He was on 21 days sick leave recovering in hospital from War Wounds. I was a nurse looking after many patients. John grabbed my attention every moment he could. When it was peaceful one afternoon he took me into his arms, looking passionately at my lips and said 'Dawn I love you', his voice so sincere, so husky, so sexy. I just melted in his embrace. Six months later when his ship docked we were married. In war time it was impossible to buy an engagement ring therefore my mother gave me hers, it served a dual purpose and good fortune went along with it."

The dear lady seemed to be happy with what she said, perhaps it was the first time she'd told it. Vic takes Jenny's hand; holding it firmly he saw her willingness to take the ring. Full of pride and confidence he tenderly slips the ring onto her finger he bows to kiss both the ring and her finger affectionately.

The Lesser Evil

He said aloud for all to hear, "Jenny I love you. Taking this ring makes our betrothal absolute."

John passes champagne to each, lifts his glass and joyously said, "To Vic and Jenny, may they both find good health and happiness in their future life together"…

During the ensuing conversation with the two lovers, John mentioned that he had a pleasant surprise for them both. Suddenly a musician holding a mandolin came to their table to ask if Jenny would request a number from a prepared list of tunes he'd passed to her. She chose the first one an old Italian slow waltz tune 'Maria lana'. He would be happy to dedicate it to her. It was one of his favourites also. The Balalaika band had played this particular number often before… When the first strains of the music were heard many took to the dance floor… The blending of the stringed instruments in perfect harmony, the soft cascading and gently swelling tune fitted the waltz temp beautifully. The party mood is happy, romantic… infectious… Vic's holding Jenny closely, their steps match correctly. He pulls her close to him and she sees and feels his excitement. Their eyes meet in recognition and understanding of each other' feelings… Their action's slow, they cuddle and shuffle as in a dream… The music stopped… Before anybody could leave the floor the music started up again with a much faster stirring tempo 'Hungarian Folk dance' tempo. Those with energy and enthusiasm took to the floor again. Jenny griping Vic's hand and looking to leave said, "Please take me outside, it's now hot and stuffy in here, I must have a breath of fresh air…"

The late summer had been consistently hot. The night air warm with a wisp of a breeze invigorated them. A full moon shone in the distance sky well above the horizon, it's silvery lights reflecting from the gently rippling sea. He loosened his tie to open his shirt. Jenny released her hair allowing it to flow over her shoulders; she ruffles it, the cooling air felt nice. She kicks off her shoes…throws her arms up to heaven emphasising her beautiful breast and figure. Taking Vic's hand they briskly walk across the road to the beach. The night is silent, nothing stirs. The sea air is refreshing it stimulates and heightens their senses. Vic sees moon beams twinkle in her eyes. He feels her excitement… Instinctively they know what to do. Hurriedly they shed their clothes leaving everything

132

on the glistening dry sand. Hand in hand they ran vigorously free and naked. Like children they ran over the deserted beach and to the warm calm shallow sea, continuing into deeper water. They were unconscious of everything except each other. He wanted her physically. His arm tightened around her waist.* She responded to him wrapping her arms around his shoulders. Their bodies pressed together beneath the warm sea water. They kissed. It was a hungry kiss, it stirred the passion within them. It lingered about them and prompted the fire that buried in them both. It triumphed over them reaching down to the soul of them.

She moved her thighs against him, searching for his awakened sex. He gasped when he felt himself cleave into her as she raised herself to receive him. He kissed her savagely to stop himself crying out at the flood of pleasure, pain and relief of passion. She held him tightly, trembling with excitement at her own relief and joy with him. They stayed locked together for all the world as if they were one…

Slowly they became aware of the water. They moved to swim together. Jenny rolled to take him with herself under the water surface. They stood in shallow water laughing because they felt free of all worldly anxieties.

"It's wonderful, just wonderful being in love", she said and moved from the sea to the dry sand. Their eyes were adjusting to the moon light, everything seemed clearer. He stood gazing at her exquisite figure as she eased from him… She turned her face toward him. The moonlight seemed to focus upon her loveliness. Impulsively he's drawn to her. He came near to take her, she turned away and ran along the beach knowing he would chase after her; that he would catch up with her and they would fall together and make love again. Watching her stride, she ran gracefully like a gazelle, he easily ran close not intending to get ahead of her, he was excited by her beautiful muscular rhythm… Suddenly she stopped, turned, stood firm with her arms outstretched to receive him. He willingly fell full force into her embrace. Their hearts beating with excitement, their lips and bodies combined as they fall to their knees in humble surrender to each other. She offered her luscious lips, they kissed as she manoeuvred herself to lay upon the hard sand. He went with her

---

* Her nakedness greatly hightened his excitement.

133

every move and again they made love without any inhibition, twisting their bodies in desire to give each other ecstatic pleasure...and fulfilment. She knew that she belonged to him now... Vic stood, looking down, Jenny laying like Venus Goddess of Love in every way beautiful. What had he ever done to deserve her love?

"Jenny you look exquisitely lovely." She sat up threw her hair back, offered her hand... Helping Jenny to her feet he pulls her to his breast... expecting he would do that she melts in his arms. They stood for a while like a statue mentally and physically caressing each other...totally committed lovers. With their arms around each other they walk slowly from the inflowing tide to gather their clothes. Sparsely dressed they sneak into the hotel. Everything is quiet as they enter their room. Jenny goes straight to the window to look out across to the beach where they had made love. She wanted to embellish the memory and the scene upon her mind for ever.

They both enjoyed a long day into the night...It had been an emotional evening and night. They were tired, spent by their love they fell upon their bed to sleep in each other arms...

Beams of sunlight flooded the room and swept across the floor with the warmth of the new day. They spend their day leisurely lounging on the beach under the sun, talking and planning their life and future together.

Vic looked at her as she lays in a two piece swim suit, whilst the warm sun blesses her. She's the most desired woman he'd ever known. He took her hand and kissed each fingertip. It made her body zing with desire for him. In a dream like mind she turned to him again.

"I love you", he whispered to her. "I've never loved anyone more." She smiled, she knew without any doubt that the words came from his heart.

The Lesser Evil

REPETITIVE STRAIN

Early Monday morning Vic and Jenny left the hotel and travelled by taxi to Poole. He was expected to attend at John Hardwick's office at 10.00am. Jenny would go on to her flat to change into suitable everyday attire. They agreed to meet again in the Poole office canteen for coffee about 11.00am. She would drive her car to the car park over looked from the canteen south window. John Hardwick, acting in his official capacity as Western district Commander, gave Vic application forms for employment as a trainee customs officer. They completed the forms together, after discussing Vic's career prospects. Vic signed his part and John signed the recommendation… Vic would be interviewed by two additional officers next day.

John smiling said, "I have also recommended you for a substantial special award. It specifically mentions your co-operation with our department, (lengthy statement in detail followed), you received physical injuries and suffered personal property damage and losses. The recommendation has been received by the appropriate government department and in due course an amount of cash could be awarded to you. I cannot say just how much money you could get but it's my guess that it might be perhaps £5,000. There will be no reward for surrendering the drugs you brought into the country because nothing was said about that for obvious reasons." Vic nodded his understanding.

"I'm obliged to you for putting my name forward for an award. Whatever it might amount to it will be very welcome. Also I'm pleased that you have directed my future employment opportunities. I'd never thought of being a Customs Officer before now. However, I'm sure with training I'll make the grade very soon", he said with self assured confidence.

"Part of your training will be for you to attend a Human Relations Course. That will help you become settled and understand civilian life better. The training will direct you into citizenship...you have most of the other personal qualifications to succeed."

Vic's happy because people are taking interest in his life. In thanking Mister Hardwick he had a sudden urge to salute him but stopped himself with a smile. "Thank you"...

Looking out from the canteen window, holding his coffee, he can see across the car parking area. Jenny is expected to drive in at any minute...

Jenny turned the key and entered her flat. Closing the door behind herself, her nose sensed the aroma of freshly made coffee. Speedily she moves to the kitchenette. She's shocked to find the electric kettle still warm. She senses another presence in the place. A voice, a male voice muttered:

"Jenny I'm sorry if I startled you"... She froze on the spot, panic seized her mind. She jerked her head round toward the spoken words never expecting anybody. The voice shocked and enraged her.

"Who are you? What are you doing in my flat? How did you get in here? How do you know my name?" she's perplexed!

She sped to open the curtain emitting more light. She saw a man...

"Yes, Jenny it's me, Reggie Baker", she's staggered. "I'm plastered up around my neck and head, you might not recognise me now. Brian did this to me. He just went raving mad when he saw the police cars swarming into the farm. It was my stupidity that led the police to move in upon

136

us, Brian said. Then he went into an hysterically mad rage. Sometimes he'd be very intelligent, others he'd have brain storms – go mad."

"Shut up I don't want to know. You understand, I don't want to hear any more about it. I don't believe you, get out", she screamed. Her screams were not heard outside.

Her stomach turned over. Her nerves jarring and her mind reeling in confusion... She must satisfy her mind about this intruder. He said he's Reggie Baker. How can it be? Baker or 'Lesser' was smashed up in the accident, he's dead. She moves towards him. He stands in the light anticipating her need to recognise him. His face is swollen, bruised and distorted by the stretching of skin sewn to cover his neck wounds. He's not the upright, bad tempered, dominant man she knew. He's humiliated and dangerous.

"Jenny, remember we first met at a party aboard the cruise ship Oriana?"

Feverishly he continued to bring to her mind more information and facts that only both of them would know. Her whole being is troubled taking it in, she hesitates not wanting the mental strain, it hurt her brain, she couldn't deny him.

"Alright, I can see who you are... Now what do you want?" she demanded.

Confused she cannot understand how he comes to be standing, talking in front of her. She believed him to be dead and wishes it to remain that way. He continues talking, explaining politely, pleading. She turned away not listening to half of his words. She had to recollect her thoughts and adjust her mind to this new situation, trying to put everything back in perspective.

The man she hated for so long now presents himself like a ghost from the past endeavouring to explain himself. To satisfy her curiosity she must let him speak, she must know why he invaded her privacy, her life.

He feverishly continued talking; his mouth twisted, his voice guttural, his words confused.

"When I staggered from the bungalow with blood pulsating from my neck wounds a constable rushed to my aid and so did you Jenny. I told the police that 'He was getting away. They believed that meant me, the man they came for, was escaping. An ambulance car rushed me from the farm to the hospital because I was bleeding profusely. I told the hospital nurse my name's Brian Boothe. The surgeon operated upon me immediately to arrest the bleeding. I was in the outpatients department when a man was brought in supposedly suffering from cuts, bruises and a broken shoulder blade. He was telling the doctor that a maniac driving a lorry at reckless speed crashed into the land tractor that he was using. The impact force threw him from the tractor some yards up the track to land on his shoulder. He believed the trucker died in the accident. Hearing his story I concluded that Brian had been killed in that collision, I suddenly thought it safe to take his identity, to allow everybody to believe that I am Brian Booth. The police were eager to arrest Reggie Baker. If they believed he died in the crash they would no longer be looking for him" he said. "I was retained in the hospital three days. The ward sister told me that a Police constable would be arriving about midmorning to get a statement from me to do with my neck lacerations etc. I had no desire to be interviewed by a police constable. It could be that they had discovered my true identity so I decided to leave. I stole a hooded garment from the hospital staff cloakroom and sneaked away to arrive here in your flat about half an hour ago. I used a plastic business card to get past the door lock. It's easy."

Looking at him she sees a more sinister and lesser man than he'd previously been, he's not able to make demands upon anybody now. His rackets are finished, his criminal empire collapsed. His partners in crime are in jail, dispersed or dead. She no longer felt threatened by his presence in her flat. She was about to order him out when he said:

"Jenny, I am a desperate man, the police will be looking for me. You're the only one I can turn to for help… You must help me. I'll reward you handsomely when I get to the boat quay at Poole… I have my power boat in the Marina there. In the safe there's sufficient money. I'll will give you a thousand pounds in bundles of fifty pound notes for you to discreetly get me to board my boat. I'll have little need for cash at sea. I promise you will hold the money as I speed away."

"Most of my money is banked in Jersey and Luxembourg, you understand?"

138

Jenny listened, contemptuous of his words and promises, scornful of his ill gotten money offer, but afraid of the consequences if she refused to help. Thinking to phone the police, she saw his anger and aggression would stop her before she dialled the number. Lesser could see the hesitation on her face, he placidly said:-

"Jenny, I've always had a soft spot for you ever since I first saw you. I know you thought me too old and perhaps a little brash, I always tried to be pleasant and kind to you. Of course I'd never hurt you. Jenny it's a once only urgent request. You must help me get aboard my boat. I have no money, no friends, only you." Jenny's mind is racing ahead of her. She knows he'd not hurt her unless it was in desperation. She's suffering under duress and would be pleased to see him disappear. Overcoming her reluctance to do anything to help him, she asked, "What is it you want of me?"

"Take me in your car to the Poole quay Marina. You'll leave your car there. I'll show you where to park. We'll walk together passing the security post. I'll have the hood over my head to hide the bandages. It should seem natural to anybody, a man and a woman going to their boat. We'll need to walk along to jetty number 5 to board my boat. That's not too much to ask for a thousand pounds is it?"

"Before I drive into Poole Marina I'll be going through the town", she said.

"I'll keep my head covered and simply be seen as your passenger. I should attract nobody's attention. You must not stop on route except for traffic control, go straight to the quay. I'll give you directions."

Jenny has butterflies in her belly. Realising that she will be passing the entrance to the Customs house offices car park where Vic could be waiting.

"I'll have to change into something more suitable", she entered the bedroom closing the door firmly from her side against intruders. She's trembling with fear, there's no escape.

Lesser tensed with anxiety and apprehension will do anything necessary to get away on to his boat. He enters the kitchen. Sorting through the cutlery he steels a knife with an 8 inch long blade drawn to a sharp point. He sees this as a suitable weapon. Wrapping the blade in a tea towel he puts it into the inner breast pocket of his coat. It might be useful if he has to persuade Jenny or anybody to do his will.

Jenny reappears dressed in a tracksuit, ready to meet any situation. Lesser, smiling at her said, "Jenny, again you're a fine figure of a woman even in that getup."

She did not cherish his complements. She still harboured resentment and sought vengeance against him. She had no intent to do his bidding or take his money and must always be alert to any possible dirty tricks that he might conjure up. Jenny realised she will be the only person to witness his departure and this gave her cause for concern. She is however relieved to know Lesser's eager to get away and that will be the last of him but she's no faith in the notion.

It's about 15 minutes drive to the quay. Road traffic moved steadily. Near the town centre she notices a foot patrol constable. She could stop by the police man get out of the car and tell the constable she's being molested. Lesser also saw the police man. He saw in her face what she was thinking. The car slowed to a near walking pace. Lesser, with evil intent, pressed the point of the sharp blade into Jenny's left side to leave no doubt of his intention.

"Don't even think about stopping. If I have to I'll thrust this blade through your rib and into your heart. You'll be dead in a minute. Drive on steadily, it's about 2 miles where you will turn left into the quay road. Jenny felt the point of the blade; it did not puncture the skin. Now she knows he's dangerous, hostile and determined to proceed ahead. There seems to be no avoiding his determination to get aboard his boat...

Vic Brandon is impatiently waiting by the entrance to the car park. He expected Jenny to drive in more than half an hour ago. 'Something's wrong' he thought. She wouldn't be so late unless something important has delayed her. He's suffering, eager to tell her about his successful meeting with John Hardwick. He's to become a trainee customs officer and in due course will get a four figure award. He's watching the traffic moving. He sees at a visual distance a white Mercedes car. It's Jenny. His heart skips a beat at the sight of it. At last she's come. But she's not alone another hooded person sits in the front seat with her. He's worried, puzzled, confused. Who can it be? He stands aside to give clear passage for the car
140

to turn into the parking lot. It makes no sign of any such move. Expecting to see the traffic indicator flash, he saw instead the car's hazard warning lights flashing. Jenny placed her left hand across her forehead to indicate pain and distress. He distinctly saw a sparkle of sunlight from her engagement ring as the car passed within a few feet from him. In a state of nervous anxiety and utter confusion he believes she conveyed to him a warning of pain and hazard ahead.

Vic stepped into the open road to see the car indicating to turn about 300 yards ahead in to the quay road. This is his chance, the road down to the quay is one way only in and out, there's no turn off. He starts running with ever increasing intensity in his stride. The car stops for a minute to allow two cars to come onto the main road, Jenny saw in the rear view mirror Vic chasing at a distance behind. The knife point in her side forcedly urges her to proceed. Lesser is watching every move she makes… He's not seeing her lover running furiously to catch up. It's nearly a mile down the road to the Marina.

Jenny slows down to allow Vic to get a little closer… Lesser tells her to accelerate. She thinks it's a speed restricted road, the knife point dominates the argument. … The car speeds up a little; the harbour's in sight. Lesser points to a space used principally for the launching of trailer born boats,

"Stop the car there, that space next to the launch ramp and get out of the car. I'll be close to watch every move you make. No tricks now I don't want to leave a dead body by your car."

Lesser takes Jenny's arm. The knife point is hidden under his coat. He steers her along the quayside to jetty 5. Everything's still and quiet, nobody is about. Lesser has not seen Vic racing down to the quay. She is apprehensive, fears being kidnapped again. She is resisting, attempting to slow their pace. She senses and fears his evil intent. He's not leaving any witness to his departure…

Lesser, so near to his escape boat, drags Jenny twisting, turning, kicking and fighting like a wildcat. He has a fierce grip of her. She reels her body violently round in an attempt to lose them their balance and topple them both into the water. He counteracts gripping a handful of her hair wrenching her head backwards. She blindly tears at his face with her fingernails. Getting a firm hold of his neck bandage she pulls and twists it desperately tearing open his wounds. His agonizing pain causes the knife to fall through the open slat wooden decking upon which they struggle. The boat alongside is low in the water. In their tussle, he misses his step looses balance and together they fall down hard to roll onto the boat deck. The violent shock reaction and concussion to Jenny's head leaves her semi-conscious, unable to make coherent affective resistance. Lesser drags her down to the cabin, shoves her inside and locks the hatch. Blood from his open wounds oozing out into his clothing and onto the lower step.

Hurriedly he climbs up onto the control deck and starts the engines...

Vic Brandon ran the mile down to the quay like a racetrack greyhound, with fury in his heart and soul, he's desperately determined to succeed. He must get to Jenny. He knows he feels she's in dire need of help. She's being taken by a mysterious tyrant. Vic turns along at the end of the quay to see a cabin type cruiser power boat leaving its berth, manoeuvring to go out to sea. There's no time for a second breath. He must get onto that boat. He's sure Jenny's taken captive; he opens his stride straining every sinew in his body. His heart pounding madly, he's determined to achieve his aim...

The boat moves up alongside the jetty gaining headway out of the harbour...

Vic Brandon's running furiously, enters the wooden jetty reckoning that within about 30 strides the boat will pass it's end...He can make it.

The power boat gaining speed makes Vic strive. His stamina is sure, he summons up the blood and leaps from the extreme end of the jetty... The boat at that point has adequate clearance... swiftly leaping out into the distance with his right arm outstretched to the boats port side he grabs the centre gunnel rave, holding fast his feet in the water being dragged by the speeding craft. The current helps him to move alongside to a rear position where the boat dips, it's easier to lift his legs to climb aboard, he's made it.

He heaves a deep breath of satisfaction but cannot relax...

The boat's set on a straight course speeding out from the harbour. Vic stands to see a man hurriedly stumbling down a few steps from the control deck. Enraged and limping, holding a crowbar with a hooked claw end clasped in his right hand, he lunges at his intruder. Vic seeing it coming swiftly parries it aside and came in close seeing his assailant's blooded face... He's profoundly shocked and momentarily stunned... the face distorted, blood encrusted loose bandage around his neck, he's looking at the face of a ghost. The evil eyes he will never forget. They're the eyes of the evil Lesser staring menacingly at him with murderous expression across his grim jaw. Vic shies away. Suddenly his assailant jabs the hooked end of the bar he wielded into Vic's groin with force enough to cause him to double up in pain...with the iron bar held at each end Lesser crashes it down. Vic anticipated it was aimed at his head, he jerked himself forward, the blow fell on his back causing him to fall flat on his face. Vic has no weapon, he fears the heavy crow bar. He must wrestle the dangerous cosh from his attacker. His nose on the deck, he sees only his enemy's foot coming into attack. He grabs the ankle wrenching the leg toward himself, putting Lesser off balance, causing him to lean and fall backward to recover his stance. Vic, holding fast to his ankle, is lifted partly aiding his own recovery. Standing firm, in a flash he bought his right fist with force into direct contact with Lesser's lower jaw just as he was poised to strike again. The punch staggered him and he dropped the weapon on the deck. It was a knockout blow... somehow he sustained it. He reacted in a temper and kicked Vic's knee cap. Pain spasms shot up and down his leg, paralysing and crippling him. Unsteady he fell forward onto the triumphant Lesser. Immediately he stood adroit and furiously head butted his opponent's nose sending pain and shock waves right through his brain to the nape of his neck. His whole body shook in a nervous tantrum; he went into mad uncontrolled rage, shouting obscenities into the sky. Possessed of evil and with his remaining strength he viciously thrust himself at Vic with both arms and fingers outstretched ready to strangle the life out of his throat. In a split second Vic plunged his head down into Lesser's stomach. The impact took the wind out of him and he fell bent over Vic's head and back. In the same instance he grabs Lesser's waist belt lifting him partly, sending him clear over his back to fall with his body weight square upon his forehead. The crash stunned him. He's not likely to recover from that quickly...

The Lesser Evil

Jenny soon shook off the effects of her heavy fall... She's no longer dazed but finds herself locked inside the cabin. She can hear the fighting and thumping on the aft deck. In fair fight she's not worried about Vic's ability to ward off his attacker. She is however afraid of Lesser's dirty tricks. She must, therefore get out to help as best she can. She finds a heavy metal cylinder fire extinguisher; using it like a battering ram particularly on the area of the hatch lock. The thing started to discharge white foam impeding her efforts. Soon she smashes her way out to put her foot on the first exit step-up out of her prison.

Vic sees her emerging from the cabin and speeds to her aid. She has foam in her hair and on her clothing that in no way deters them. He lifts her into his arms. She's so pleased to see that he's is not seriously hurt; she offers her lips and they remain in an embrace hugging and kissing. Lesser's no match for a healthier and younger man: blood is oozing from his neck wound, he will not engage in any further physical contests; other ideas storm his mind.

He takes up the crowbar and hurriedly smashes open the boat's emergency equipment locker and grabs a signal flare gun; he cocks the action... Intending to fire it at the back of Vic's head in retaliation... Vengeance seizes his brain; gloating and grinning like a maniac he lifts the flare gun, released the safety catch, and deliberately points it at his target...

Jenny secure in Vic's arms, snug in his shoulder, sees Lesser raise the weapon to fire it at them. Her reaction; swifter than the missiles spinning toward them; in a flash she stamped hard on Vic's toe. His natural reaction was to bend down to that pain; she pushed and fell with him to the ground. The projectile whizzed over their bodies with only a small clearance leaving behind it a trail of flaring magnesium smoke. It wizzed on further through the open hatch to be stopped in collision with the cabin's bunk bed-sofa. The flare continues burning profusely spluttering flames in various directions...

Vic Brandon stands up sharply, anger coursed through his veins. Now he knows that he's dealing with an insane murdering maniac with intent to destroy both of them.

Lesser, still holding the flare gun, looks at them both standing unhurt. He's full of anger, stamping, infuriated and regretting having failed to hit

144

his target... he must try again. The fire in the cabin has taken hold and is burning fiercely. In his disarranged crazy state of mind it seems Lesser doesn't notice the fire but moves instead to recharge the flare gun.

Vic must stop a second attempt to assassinate them, he must take the infernal gun from Lesser's hand even if he has to break his arm to get it. The mad man turns to get another flare rocket. Vic leaps with great agility and is upon him before he lifted the locker lid. Grabbing his right wrist in a powerful grip he twists his arm up behind his back toward his neck and at the same time swung his arm around Lesser's throat forcing his head back in a wrestle like hold. The flare gun fell from his grasp and Vic kicked it across the deck out of reach. Fearfully aware of the cabin fire flaring out of control he orders Jenny to get the remaining flares and throw them up the bow of the boat. Vic, holding his captive firmly, drags him back away from the locker to give Jenny clear access. As she passes near to them Lesser jerks and turns against his captor's hold: thrusting his boot out, kicking Jenny hard in her leg just under the knee cap, bringing her down to the deck in pain; at the same time punched Vic in his right side. Before Vic could regain control, Lesser with renewed strength, forces himself back against his head lock hold. Speedily he lifts both his legs up high and together brought them down to stamp with the heels of his boots upon Vic's toes. That really hurt. This caused Vic to release his arresting hold over Lesser who turned away and ran toward the cabin fire, his bleeding unarrested... Jenny stood up, her pride more hurt than the bruise on her leg; assured Vic that she was alright and proceeded to dump the flare rockets out of reach. She looked at the cabin blazing and said aloud,

"With a flare up like that we are in danger, we'd better get off this boat now!."

Vic saw that the speeding boat caused a wind to feed the flames. He looked up to Jenny to help him get the life raft out of the locker.

"We'll soon have to abandon ship", he said.

"We could not launch an inflatable life dinghy whilst the boat is speeding over the waves and we'd never be able to get into it", Jenny said.

"You're right; somehow I'll have to stop the engines."

The Lesser Evil

Vic takes up the crowbar and moves steadily to the rear of the boat. He finds two high powered outboard motors revving at full throttle. He calls Jenny to hold his coat tail whilst he stretches over the stern end to reach the fuel supply lines. With perfect balance and dexterity he used the crowbar as a lever to sever the main fuel pipe. Both engines stopped in less than a minute... The boat ceased pushing against the waves and petrol flows freely upon the sea... Vic lept, strove and fought to get aboard that boat to take Jenny from her abductor. He knew the risk he was taking, she's worth it, he's now taking her off. As they launch the inflated life raft onto the choppy sea, he hears and sees Lesser shouting, raving like a lunatic whilst thrusting his outstretched arms to the sky. The demented fool is dancing upon the fragile roof of the control cabin. Under his feet there's a ravaging inferno. Vic takes Jenny, helping her into the small life raft, as they drift away they hear the cracking and see the caving in of the cabin roof upon which Lesser danced. Flames belched out vigourously as Lesser descended into the fire beneath him and into the arms of Mephistopheles... The flames change to dark red and swirling smoke towered up into the sky. A weird wailing wind stirred around the pyre scene.

The distant coast line is scarcely visible as Vic rowed the dingy toward the land. Jenny sat looking at her hero rowing away with inadequate oars; she spoke of her gratitude, giving him every encouragement. The going is tediously slow, they will never make land before nightfall. He stopped rowing looking at the boat they'd left burning in the near distance... It'll burn out eventually and sink, he thought... suddenly flaming debris shot out of the craft in every direction. Scattering bits all around to fall back onto the surface of the sea around them, smoke towered high in to the sky. The fuel tank exploded with great force blowing the boat apart and setting fire to the fuel floating upon the sea. Jenny turned sharply to see and hear the big bang, she became transfixed, repulsion choked her, the scene engulfed her mind... she wrenched her eyes and mind away as quickly as she could and shook her head in abject horror at what she had seen. She put her face into her cupped hands and sobbed convulsively... it was a relief of mental and physical pain and exhaustion... He didn't try to console her, Jenny had suffered a lot with Lesser; she had to get it all

146

out of her system… Turning, he looked aghast as the last smouldering embers sink beneath the waves.

Vic looked around from horizon to horizon, there was nothing now to see, everything was deadly quiet… They felt bewildered in a great sea with no means of communication, they could drown and nobody would know. Jenny lifted her head, looked with staring eyes into the sky. She's relieved of all stress and anxiety later.

"Do you hear that?" she asked Vic. "It sounds like thunder. Ho! not a summer storm, we could be drowned." She strains her ears. "It's a helicopter to the rescue." The coast guard had seen the fire in the distance and came to investigate.

Hovering closely over the scene, they searched the area but found no body.

Half an hour later the coast guard team winched them aboard the machine and took them to the naval hospital at Portland for a medical check up. Both suffered nothing more serious than cuts, abrasions and bruises. They were each given sedatives and embrocation to rub into their aches and pains. John Hardwick heard about their adventures at sea and asked James Gordon to take them both to his hotel. They were advised to talk to nobody about their adventure and rescue. Boats sometimes catch fire at sea and sink without a trace.

They couldn't wait to get into their bedroom. Jenny saw her reflection in a mirror. She looked a mess and felt it. She dropped her clothing stepping naked into the shower cabinet. Her flesh cringed and crept as cascading warm water relieved her of all anxiety and tension.

Eagerly smothering herself with a bottle full of bath gel to vigorously clean her body, to rid her hair of fire foam and to cleanse her mind and soul of the whole evil experience of the last hurtful hours. Vic stood watching her, she's enthusiastically scrubbing herself determined to be no longer tarnished by the evil of Lesser; the memories she'd banished from her mind. The final deluge of clear clean water gave her the ultimate relief she earnestly sought. Heaving a deep breath, a sigh of relief she turns; Vic's holding out a great bath towel for her to step into. He was still patting her dry as she took a few paces to fall flat, face down, naked upon the bed. She asked Vic to get the embrocation and apply it to her

147

bruises; one mark on her left upper arm; the other on the left cheek of her bum reaching to her hip joint, both bruises as big as the palm of his hand.

"Jenny its my pleasure to massage ointments into your lovely body. I fear I might get over zealous and perhaps hurt you".

"I want you to massage me. We'll both get pleasure from it. I know you will be gentle. I'm sure you'll love doing it for me, as I'll do it for you."

Vic's eyes swept over her every curve from head to heel, her lovely long legs, perfect in every muscle, her whole body perfect in every form. He became excited just looking at her. Rolling up his shirt sleeves to give himself better reach he applies the unction to her warm soft wounded body, willingly, softly, smoothly and gently easing the pains out of her. He worked leisurely, persistently to give her of his best effort. She laid quiet and still, in her peace of mind and state of tranquillity. She drifted into sleep...

He's pleased that his nimble fingers had such a calming effect upon her tortured body and soul... carefully without waking her he places a bed cover over her. Collecting her shed clothing, he takes each item to be cleaned. Earlier that morning when they left the hotel together neither could have imagined they'd be brought back to the hotel after a perilous dramatic escapade at sea.

Vic never mentions to the receptionist anything about their recent experiences, he did however get everything cleaned, dried and suitable for her to wear again later... In the meantime he returned to the bedroom. Jenny had turned in her sleep breathing heavily, he would not waken her. Quietly he slipped into the shower; the warm cascading water flowing over his body greatly eased his aches and pain of the recent conflict.

Vic checked himself over: he'd sustained no damage to his head wounds. Realising that he was lucky to have been able to snatch Jenny from a kidnapping he decides to put the whole adventure out of his mind as best he could at that time. He remembers somebody saying: "Nothing cleans the body and soul better than soap and water." As he's soaping his body, creating a purging lather, the soap tablet slips from his fingers falling outside the shower basin. He moved to retrieve it, reaching down whilst

148

still standing in the booth; his eyes not clear, fumbling for the tablet, it's put into his hand. He stood up wiping his eyes seeing Jenny bring her eager lips to his, her nakedness to him… They embrace each other and explore all the pleasures passionately. They enjoy each other sexually… The shower head above raining down warm water over them, enhancing their sex drive. They go into an all consuming, loving sexual rage, totally exhausting them. She knows how to please him… and he her!…

Stepping from the shower, into a bath robe, Vic wraps Jenny in a bath coat towel, and picks her up into his muscular arms. She loves her powerful hero sweeping her off her feet; she'd surrender her whole life to him…

"There's somebody at the door", she said.

Placing her upon the bed he attends to the caller.

"Room Service", said a school girl. "I've brought up the lady's washing and cleaned her shoes".

"Thanks", said Vic, he gave her a few coins. Jenny nodded her head in approval… Looking up to him she whispered in a sexy voice "Vic come back here!…"

The evening sky shone bright and colourful when they awoke from their slumbers. They'd both recovered from their ordeal, aches and pains forgotten.

"That's the only clothing I have here. I can't go down to dinner in a track suit."

"We could have our dinner brought up to our room."

"No thank you", she said with a determined voice. "Do you know what I'd like?" She gave the answer in the same breath. "I'd love to walk the sea front promenade under the beautiful coloured light, sit at an open air café table, eat from the menu, drink exotic wine and watch the moon rise over the gently rippling sea, that's romantic, that's for me"

The Lesser Evil

THE TIDE TURNS

The following morning they arrived by taxi at Poole quay, first to collect her car and to take Vic to his career interview. Vic agreed to meet her later for lunch at the Commodore restaurant… Before attending his scheduled interview Vic called in to briefly speak with John Hardwick. He'd received a police report about Vic's car. They found the car had been fitted with a small heat sensitive plastic capsule very near the exhaust pipe. Within a few minutes of the engine running the plastic melts releasing cyanide gas to be taken into the car by the car's warm air ventilating system. The cyanide gas is lethal, in this case intended to kill the car driver after travelling only a short distance. Inhaling the gas would make the driver unconscious and induce death whilst accelerating the car to the detriment of others using the road. Vic read the report, contemplating the intent shook him. What evil mind thought of that? The gas capsule was meant to kill him. He soon shrugged off the effect, he has to attend to more important business.

"Mr VICTOR JOHN BRANDON." His full name read out from a document placed upon a table in front of two men and a woman seated to consider his future.

"You're an applicant for employment as a trainee customs officer. Is that correct?"

"Yes, that is correct. That's me", Vic said with determination and confidence in his voice.

150

V J Tarry

The apparent senior of the two men said, "We have favourable reports both from the War office about your military service, another from the local commander John Hardwick." They're impressed with his career and enthusiasm, his appointment now seems to be a forgone conclusion. "We also understand that you're not settled in civil life yet."

Vic's response, "that's correct I am not settled."

"Do you understand that if you are offered employment you will be a civil servant and that you may be required to serve anywhere your service is needed. That could be any post in the British Empire?"

Vic Brandon understood every word said, further he could see the intentions of the panel. They read of his ability to act upon his own initiative, his foresight, planning and many more achievements edging onto recent adventurous activities favourable to the Customs Service of which they're forbidden to give official recognition. After some talk between themselves they agreed to offer him Gibraltar as his first training station. He would have to attend an induction course; amongst other things he will learn Civil Service procedures. His basic training could be about a month's duration. It would deem a suitable posting taking into consideration his involvement in recent dramatic events yet to be resolved in the highest courts... effectively they'd be pleased to see the back of him.

Vic was required to attend The Civil Service training college with expenses and accomodation provided. He discussed his interview with Jenny at their lunch.

"Is that for sure? I mean you're being sent to Gibraltar in about four weeks", Jenny asked. She glowed with delight at the thought; it's a gateway to Europe she loved. "We'll have frequent opportunity to travel the Continent"

"Yes, after I complete my initial training."

"I'm going with you. I shall apply for a transfer to Gibraltar immediately. I feel sure that it will be cleared through and we can go together", Jenny said with enthusiasm. She had travelled to Spain and Gibraltar on cruise ships and she knew the rock well, she's fluent in the Spanish language. Gibraltar could be a perfect posting. Two days later Jenny put her bid in to be transferred to Gibraltar, it was granted three weeks into Vic's training course perhaps for the same reason they wished to send Vic there.

151

The Lesser Evil

It was late evening when Vic's train pulled into the station. He'd returned from a five week successful completion of an intensive training course. Jenny met him as he walked from the main entrance. She drove straight to her flat. They'd both have so many things to talk about, they missed each other terribly.

Previously Vic returned for a weekend leave and travelled on to the sea front hotel with a view across the beach to the open sea. Jenny loved this place, it would always be like a honeymoon hotel for both of them…

Her car stopped at the front entrance of the residence building in which she has her flat, with a naughty twinkle in her eye, a smile upon her lips and surprise written across her face, she said :-

"Vic, the last time we stood together upon this doorstep I'd forbade you entrance then. We both knew what would happen if I'd let you in. I saw your disappointment and I'm sure you understood. I felt so mean to have left you there … So much has happened since then … Now it's different."

Jenny takes from her pocket, two keys, she offered one to him:- "That one gives you entrance to this door, the other will give you entrance to my flat. Please take me inside, you will never be denied me again, you will always have my heart and soul."

Vic drops everything, his hands free he opens the door, scoops up Jenny into his arms taking her inside to the lift. When he returns with his baggage she's waiting, the lift open to take them higher.

He turns the second key takes his love up into his arms slowly presses the door open moving inside. She murmurs in a low voice; "I love you. Tonight I will dare anything … Take me through to my bedroom …

It might have been more than an hour later when he woke up with the smell of sizzling hot prime steak in his nostrils. Jenny planned an at home dinner for themselves with candlelight and rich red wine, beautifully laid out in banquet style. She'd learnt a thing or two whilst cruising. Vic enjoyed every morsel, their excellent dinner paving the way to her man's heart, he loved it!

Vic remained in his accommodation until his transfer posting came up. He was told that a flat will be ready for him upon his arrival in Gibraltar. It was discreetly understood that Jenny would be accommodated at the same address. She gave up her place with the understanding that she will vacate at the end of the month. In the post Jenny received a cheque for a lot of money. The insurance company eventually paid out on her deceased husband's business policy. Vic received his first month's pay and expenses likely to be incurred whilst travelling. The police training school purchased his old car to use as a training aid. They had dismantled the car looking for booby traps and thought it uneconomical to rebuild. Vic and Jenny arranged to sail aboard the car ferry from Weymouth to Cherbourg, France and from there onward they'd travel by her car leisurely through Spain to Gibraltar, stopping about halfway overnight at some small cosy romantic hotel.

The day before they were to leave Vic and Jenny were required to attend John Hardwick's office for final briefing. He expressed sorrow and regret at loosing Jenny. He praised Vic for his courage, foresight and considerable help, most of which was to remain unofficially recognised.

Jenny said, "I'm sure you must know that Vic saved me from being kidnapped."

John speedily placed his hand gently to Jenny's mouth to stop her saying more upon the subject. He was fully aware of the accidental boat fire at sea over a month ago and that the coastguards had dealt with the incident. They were told that everything had been made ready to receive them at their new station. A letter of introduction was given into Vic's hand, along with a new passport acquired for him whilst away.

John, smiling with shining eyes said to Vic, "I'm allowed to tell you that you have been granted a substantial award with entry in your records in citation for special services to our department, I think you will find that more acceptable than another medal? The money will be paid into your account before the end of the month."

John stood up and offered his hand, "Congratulation, It's been a great pleasure and an interest to know you, also you brought a little excitement into this office, thank you."

The Lesser Evil

Vic saw sincerity in John's face and was touched by his words. Jenny, full of pride turned upon her heel and hugged Vic closely, kissed him and turned the occasion into a congratulation ceremony. She felt so happy for him and for herself...After an awkward pause... Jenny said, "I'm sorry I forgot to return the ring."

She was slipping it from her finger when John said, "No, I'm sure my wife Dawn wished you to keep the ring. It will be good for you both and bring you good luck in your new lives together. There's a world out there, Go for it. Goodbye."

It was a beautifully sunny morning, not a cloud in the sky as Jenny drove her white Mercedes car loaded with their baggage into the lower car deck of the ferry boat that would take them to France and from there onto their future.

Upon the turn of the tide they sailed away.

Jenny and Vic stood together upon the promenade aft deck resting upon the rail holding hands seeing England recede in the distance. The boat gathered speed. Vic looks into Jenny's eyes, he felt emotional, choking in his throat, hesitated and said, "I'm the luckiest man alive, I'm the luckiest man in love." He felt her hand grip his firmly, he saw in her face she understood the feeling's mutual. Vic Brandon stepped back a pace, heaves a deep breath and feels the sea breeze in his hair. He's full of hope, expectation and enthusiasm for their life together. Grinning with self assured confidence he faces Jenny and said, "Now that the Evil Lesser affair is behind us I'm going to write a book."

THE END